Other Titles by Keith R. Rees

Legend Upon the Cane - FICTION
Quill and Ink - POETRY

The Brazilian

By
Keith R. Rees

4

For my brother, and fellow adventurer, John.

Introduction

In the summer of 1970, the country of Brazil triumphed in the World Cup football tournament that was held in Mexico City. The Brazilian football club were led by the outstanding play of their national hero, Pelé. He led them to a jubilant victory over Italy, four goals to one. It was the third World Cup victory for the Brazilians in four tries. The victory set off excited celebrations all over the country and among Brazilian football fans around the world. The Brazilian team was the first ever to accomplish three victories at the World Cup. Their incredible feat entitled them with the honor of permanently keeping the prized Jules Rimet Trophy.

Four days earlier, the Brazilians had to get past the talented national team from Uruguay. They trailed early, but fought back and won the frantic semi-final match, three goals to one. That same summer day of June 17th, a young Brazilian man had just returned from a historic journey. His name was Rodrego Ouliveyra. As the country rallied around their national team, young Rodrego gladly returned to his homeland and his anxiously awaiting family. Before his incredible odyssey, he was a simple neighborhood boy growing up in Brasilia. All he ever dreamed about was playing football. He loved to play the game and was especially excited during the days of the World Cup. Unbeknownst to his fellow countrymen, he had just completed a journey of principle and self-discovery. Little did he or anyone else know the importance of his task. A task he had been put upon unwillingly, but in the end, he would find it to be the journey of a lifetime. Then he would learn the significance of his trek. Although he would largely miss the biggest event of his national pastime, he would discover the secret of his family that had been passed down from generation to generation. A secret that would cause his country's government to stop at nothing until they themselves acquired it. Now, it was his turn to discover what his family had held on to for so long.

Chapter 1

The afternoon sun grew hot in the coastal city of Salvador. It was mid-May in 1970 on the Brazilian coast. Above the dusty-brown colored villas that lined the coastal streets were the terraces that topped each building. Some were covered with clotheslines and TV antennas, while others had palm trees in large planters with various tropical plants around them. Each villa was a different shade of wind-blown dusty-beige. Occasionally, mixed in with the dull light-brown balconies, there were villas painted colorfully in bright orange or vivid red. Only a few clouds were in the bright blue sky and the sun beat down on the steamy streets and rooftops.

On top of one of the villas that lined the sloping street called Bay View Lane, an elderly man sat outside rumpled in his chair out on a small terrace. A glass of sun tea, with two fading ice cubes in the glass, sat next to him on a rickety, old metal tray. The terrace was plain with no plants or trees around. There was not even a clothesline but just a couple of old, dusty folding chairs and a small table. In front of the old man was a light brown leather satchel which appeared to be brand new. It lay on its side on the table and had a leather shoulder strap. The flap was etched with the initials 'ESB' and was held closed with a shiny belt-buckle clasp.

The old man was well into his eighties with dark wrinkled skin around his eyes. He sat sipping on his glass of tea, occasionally staring towards the sea. He breathed a heavy sigh and melted down into his chair. He looked across the table and stared at another man sitting across from him in the only other chair on the tiny terrace. His friends name was Jacomé. He was a trusted old friend that he had known for the last fifteen years.

The old man whispered to Jacomé in a raspy voice, "Do you think he is still there?"

Jacomé was nearly sixty, but still much younger than his companion. He was the father of one daughter who had left home long ago and moved to Sao Paulo. His wife had died two years before, and now he spent most of his days sitting on terraces and in bars talking to whoever would listen. Hardly anyone would pay him the attention he wanted except for his old friend, Enso.

Enso rarely left his villa anymore. His health had declined over the years and he could no longer negotiate the two flights of stairs that led to his home. So, he shuffled from room to room each day and on good days he would go out on the tiny terrace and relax in the warm sun. The sun soothed him and always calmed him as it had for the last eighty-three years in his home of Salvador. Nowadays, he had to rely on a few friends to bring him groceries from time to time each week. Down on the corner of his block, he had always known the shopkeeper, Pereira, or Perry as the locals called him by. Perry would bring Enso things from his store when he could. Other times Jacomé would bring them to him, but on this day Jacomé came to visit Enso for another reason.

"Do you think he is still with her?" Enso asked Jacomé again.

"It's hard to tell," Jacomé answered. "You haven't contacted her in so long. When was the last time you spoke to her on the phone?"

Enso continued staring at the water with a skeptical look on his face, "She probably doesn't even remember my face anymore, I'm afraid. Besides, my damn phone doesn't work anymore. Those bastards cut the line months ago." He sat staring out into nowhere for a while longer. He thought about his youth and working life as a carpenter. All those years of hard work and building things, but he never took the time to appreciate what had been given to him. He looked down at his worn hands that ached.

"You're the only person I know that can help me with this, Jacomé. You're the only one I can trust. Can you get this to him?" he asked again anxiously.

Jacomé stared at the satchel on the table. "I will try, Enso. Brasilia is a long way from here and is very large."

"Promise me you will find him before it is too late," Enso pleaded with a serious look. "I would go myself, but…"

"It's alright, friend. Don't worry yourself. I promise I will find him," Jacomé assured him. He smiled and looked across the rooftops. "Hell, Enso, this is the first time in years I've had something important to do. It's really lifting my spirits. I'm looking forward to this big adventure. Makes me feel twenty years younger just thinking about it."

Enso was glad to see that his friend was up to the task. He knew it wouldn't be easy to find his great nephew in such a large city. He hadn't seen him since he was a toddler. He knew where his sister lived in the city but had no idea if her grandson still lived with her.

"Be cautious, old friend. Don't let this out of your sight." He pushed the leather case across the table to Jacomé then he reached across to shake his hand.

Jacomé stood in line at the bus depot waiting to buy a ticket to Brasilia. He wiped sweat off his forehead. He spotted a newspaper and soda stand down from the counter. He stepped up to the counter to buy his ticket.

"Brasilia, please. Round-trip on the two forty-five," he said to the attendant. He took his bus pass and walked to the concession to buy a newspaper and a bottle of soda. He found a wooden bench along the wall in the shade and sat down with a sigh of relief. He took a long drink from the bottle and sat sprawled on the bench watching the people pass by on the sidewalk. He had just under an hour before the bus would depart.

Two benches down, a man dressed in a beige overcoat and dark fedora, sat with a newspaper. He peered over the top of the page at Jacomé then casually looked down at his paper again. At twenty minutes to three, the call was made to board the bus for Brasilia. Jacomé got to his feet and wandered over to the loading curb and waited his turn to get on the bus. With his newspaper stuffed under his arm, he carried the leather satchel with the strap flung over his shoulder and one small traveling case in his hand. The man in the overcoat walked up behind Jacomé and bumped his newspaper, knocking it to the ground.

"Oh, pardon me, sir, terribly sorry. Let me get that for you," he said picking up the paper for Jacomé.

"Ah, that's alright," Jacomé said, perturbed and somewhat agitated.

"After you, sir," the man said politely, handing the paper back to Jacomé. Jacomé stepped onto the bus and the mysterious man followed. Jacomé found a bench to himself in the middle of the bus. The man in the overcoat smiled and continued towards the back of the bus and sat alone several rows behind Jacomé. The passengers settled in for the long ride as the bus pulled away from the station. They would not arrive until early the next day.

Chapter 2

Brasilia was alive and bustling with activity. The city was in a fever pitch in anticipation of the World Cup football matches that were about to be played in Mexico. Brazil's national team was one of the top contenders in the world tournament that was held only once every four years. The national hero was Pelé, who had helped bring two World Cup titles to Brazil in 1958 and 1962. They faltered in 1966 but were poised to win their third title with a much-improved squad this year.

Children of all ages around the country played football every day with dreams of being the next star on the national team. Some were lucky enough to make it but most of them just dreamed of it. One thing that was for certain, however, was they were all eager to see their team in the next World Cup. It was almost a national holiday that lasted two weeks every four years. Countries across the globe were always excited when it came to the year of the World Cup. Thus, as it was for every kid and adult across Brazil.

On a dusty, dirt lot in the shanty neighborhoods of southern Brasilia, teenage boys ran up and down the pitch playing their afternoon match. Some neighborhood kids and even some adults stood by to watch the game. They played in old shoes and worn-out t-shirts and shorts. Some even wore their school clothes and didn't care about how dusty they became.

On one corner of the field were a small set of rickety, wooden bleachers with a few ladies and young kids sitting on them watching the boys play. Underneath the bleachers sat a young girl just over seventeen years of age. She sat on the ground in the shade reading her textbooks from school paying little attention to the game behind her. Her name was Rosa. She heard the players running behind her on the field so she turned around and looked between the bleachers and legs of spectators to see her boyfriend, Rodrego, kicking the ball perfectly down in front of the goal for his teammate to head through the net. She smiled at seeing him having fun and wasn't surprised to see him making a perfect assist as she knew he was an excellent player. Everyone knew him as Rego. Rosa chuckled to herself when she heard his teammates chanting his name after his heroic assist.

Rosa and Rego had known each other all their lives in school and in the neighborhood. She grew to love him over the years after she saw the tragedies he had to endure in his young life. His parents were murdered in a thoughtless street crime when he was only six. He lived with his grandparents from then on. However, his grandfather died of cancer when Rego was still just a young boy at age eleven. After that tragedy occurred, his grandmother was only a shadow of herself. She sat hours upon hours in front of the TV, sometimes watching it, but most of the time simply napping in front of it. She always had her eyes closed even when she would talk to Rego. He would prepare her something to eat and bring it to her on a tray for her to nibble on while she sat in her easy chair. He never knew if she were awake or asleep since she always had her eyes closed. So, he talked to her regardless and would always leave the set on as she would grumble if he switched it off.

His grandmother, Maria, had less and less time or energy to talk with her remaining family. As her health declined, she felt embarrassed to talk to her sister and brother. She didn't want to be a bother to them, but she did feel it was her duty to watch over Rego especially. She made sure he grew up responsibly. She kept him in school and helped him with his studies, even though Rego had a poor head for study. She loved her grandson deeply and knew he tried hard despite the tragedies that he had to endure. She admired the way he faced his hardships with good humor and a zest for life.

On one occasion right after her husband died of cancer, she held Rego's hand while she sat in front of the casket. She noticed that Rego was not taking the death of his grandfather very well, so she began to cry a little and shake her head.

"Grandma, are you ok?" asked a concerned Rego.

His grandmother just smiled and continued shaking her head. "Oh Rego, I knew this day would come. He kept telling me there was something wrong with my cooking!" Rego laughed as he cried with his arms around his grandmother. She always knew how to cheer him up even at his grandfather's funeral.

It was a tough way for him to grow up, but despite everything, he faced it all courageously, which drew Rosa to him. He was her protector as well in school from the bullies that picked on her from time to time. She always did well in her studies but never looked down on him when he did poorly. Most of all, he was her dearest friend, but still she liked to torment him, in a teasing way, even though she loved him.

The game had finally ended and the players began to head to their homes. It was nearing sunset and the streets grew dark, for there were very few street lights in the neighborhood.

Rego jogged over to the bleachers and walked behind them, carrying a cup of water. "Are you in there, pretty eyes?" he called out.

"No. Go away," he heard her voice from under the bleachers. Rego peered underneath and crawled in and sat next to Rosa. "I told you not to come in here. I'm reading." she said firmly.

"What are you reading?" he asked, stretching out on the ground next to her. He was covered in sweat and his shirt was soaked through.

"None of your business," she retorted smartly.

He sat next to her and sipped from his cup of water. He stretched one knee on the ground and propped his cup on the other. He leaned over to kiss her on the cheek.

"Hey! Stop it. you're getting sweat all over me," she protested.

"You want some of my water?" he offered.

"Yes," she said quietly. He gave her the cup and she drank the rest of the water in one gulp.

"Hey, not all of it!" Rego whined. She laughed at him and gave him the empty cup. He looked at it with contempt.

"The first match for the national team is in a week," he said excitedly. "I can't wait to see it. Pelé will win it for us for sure this time. You're going to watch them with me, aren't you?"

"Yawn!"

"Ah, you'll be there. Everybody will." He crawled out from under the bleachers and started to pretend he was on the field again. *"Rego dribbles downfield, the match is tied, and time is running out! He passes to wing, the wingman lofts it back in front of the goal, and...."* He jumped into the air and acted as if he was heading an invisible ball into the nets. He threw his arms in triumph and shouted *"GOAL!!!! Brazil wins the World Cup!"* as he trotted around blowing kisses to the invisible fans. *"Rod-reeeego! Rod-reeego!"*

Rosa stopped reading her book and looked at him, shaking her head. She gathered her books and crawled out from the bleachers. "Come on Pelé, walk me home." He trotted next to her and put his arm around her.

"Get your sweaty arms off me. Here, carry these books." He grudgingly took her books and walked with her towards her home.

The sun had gone down and the streets were now dimly lit. Rosa and Rego stopped at the foot of a staircase that led to the building where her family's apartment was.

"I'll see you at seven then?" Rego asked her.

"No, eight. I have to wash my hair," she said. Rego frowned at her. He handed her the school books and leaned in to kiss her. "Not here," she said pulling back. She left him there frowning at her as she walked up the stairs and slipped inside.

15

He headed down the street and turned the corner at the next block. He walked a few more blocks then sensed someone was following him. He began to walk faster towards his building, but he still had a few blocks to go. He anxiously turned around but saw no one behind him. He looked everywhere but no one was around. He stood there for a moment shaking his head. *I must be getting paranoid*, he thought to himself.

He crossed the street and finally made it to his block when suddenly he heard a crash coming from the alley behind his building. His curiosity overwhelmed him, so he hustled over to see what was going on. He ran a few steps out into the street and slowly approached the alley. He crept near the corner and peered down the narrow passage. Suddenly, out of the darkness, came an old man with gray hair, stumbling in agony. Rego jumped in surprise as the man lurched towards him. The man's shirt was covered in blood and he tripped once more and fell right into Rego. He caught him just in time and held him up.

"Sir, are you alright? You're bleeding!" The old man tried to catch his breath, but he was in terrible pain. His eyes rolled he tried to focus on Rego.

"Oh crap, you've been *shot*," Rego exclaimed as he helped the man down to the pavement. He saw the blood all over the man's back as well. "Wait here. I have to get help!"

"No," the old man whispered. "There is no time. They'll find me."

"*Who?*" Rego asked urgently.

"Rego, you must take this," the old man said coughing. He motioned to the leather satchel still hanging from his shoulder.

Rego was stunned and confused. He hesitated for a moment and asked, "How did you know my name? Who are you?" He was feeling a bit terrified all of the sudden. Yet, he stayed focused on what needed to be done. "Please wait here. I'll get you some help, sir."

"No. You have to hurry. There is no time. You have to take this with you." Jacomé tried to pull the satchel over his shoulder but he was too weak. "Take it quickly!"

Rego sat shaking and slowly slid the strap off Jacomé's shoulder. "I need to get you some help, sir."

"No, leave me here. Rego, listen to me. Take the satchel. Take it to the Sister of St. Paul." He stopped to cough and blood spurted out onto the concreted. His head rolled back and lay against the wall.

"The what?" Rego panicked. He began to weep as he was scared out of his mind. "Sir, you need help. I need to get a doctor before it's too late," Rego wailed.

"It's already too late," Jacomé answered weakly. He lifted his head and looked straight at Rego. "You must do this, Rego. Take it to the Sister of St. Paul at Mdina. And whatever happens, never open it." His eyes rolled back in his head as he fell backwards again. His eyes closed as he coughed a few more times. Then, he breathed his last.

"Mister, wake up! What is Mdina? I don't understand! Please, you must wake up," he said sobbing.

He heard another noise coming from the alley. There were footsteps coming. He jumped and began to run down the street the other way. He stopped dead in his tracks and turned around. *The satchel! Should I go back for it?* he asked himself. A thousand thoughts raced through his mind. He quickly ran back to Jacomé where he lay dead on the pavement. He quickly grabbed the satchel and he looked at him one last time. Then, he ran down the street and around the corner and stopped to keep from view, hiding behind the corner.

The man in the overcoat came dashing out of the alley and slid to a stop when he saw the body of Jacomé lying on the ground. He pulled him away from the wall, looking all around him. Rego peered around the corner to see who it was. The man's name was Coutier. He had followed Jacomé all the way from Salvador.

"*Shit!* Where is it?" Coutier hissed under his breath

Rego quickly moved out of view. He pressed his head firmly up against the wall, his heart pounding in his chest. *Who is this man?* the question darted through his mind. He made a dash for the staircase that led to his grandmother's apartment building. The door slammed behind him. Coutier heard the door slam and ran towards the street corner. The street was empty. There were dozens of staircases that led to the residences and he could never guess which one the noise came from. He snarled under his breath. "Somebody, somewhere in these buildings *has* that case." He turned and walked away down the street, leaving Jacomé behind. He would wait until the next day to start investigating all who lived there.

Rego ran into the apartment and shut the door quickly, locking it behind him. Tears ran down his face as he looked at the leather satchel and saw the streaks of blood on it. He gazed into the room where his grandmother sat. As usual, the TV was on, but her eyes were closed. He went into the kitchen and put some water on some paper towels and wiped the blood from the satchel. He was relieved to see it came clean and did not leave a stain. He stuffed the bloodied paper towels deep into the wastebasket and went into his bedroom and closed the door. He put the satchel on a desk and quickly hopped on his bed as far away as he could get from it. He sat on the bed as his thoughts raced over in his mind everything that had just happened. He put his head down in his hands and closed his eyes, quietly sobbing to himself.

After a few moments, he gathered himself and walked into the bathroom and threw some water on his face. His grandmother never moved from her chair after he had come in. He finished washing up and put on a clean shirt. He looked at the clock in the hall and it read 7:40. Rosa was the only one he could think of to talk to about what had happened. He couldn't wait for her to come over.

Just a few minutes before eight o'clock, a knock came upon the door. Rego hurried to the door and opened it and yanked Rosa inside. He quickly did a check out in the corridor to see if anyone else was there.

"Why are you rushing me inside like that? Calm down," she protested as he closed the door behind her. She could tell something was wrong with him by the look on his face. "What's the matter?"

"*Shh,*" he whispered to her and led her to his room. They both went inside and closed the door. "I don't want her to hear."

"I didn't even get to say hello to her. She will think I am rude," Rosa said.

"It's ok, she's probably asleep anyway. I am very glad to see you," he said as he sat on the edge of his bed.

"Why? What happened? You look pale," she said, putting her hand to his forehead. She sat on the chair by his desk and saw the leather satchel sitting on it. "Where did you get this?"

"That's why I am so flipped out right now," he said finally. "Rosa, I saw a man die tonight."

"What? What are you talking about?" She knew he was serious. He joked about a lot of things, but she knew he wasn't joking about this.

"Didn't you see him by the alley? Oh man, I shouldn't have left him there!" He pressed his hands up against his forehead in panic.

"I didn't see anyone," she said emphatically. "You saw a man die? Who? You left him there?"

"I didn't have any choice," he explained. "Some crazy man was after him, so I ran away. Now he probably thinks I killed the guy. Somebody shot him, he had blood all over, and he ran right up to me!" Rosa was dumbfounded. She came across the room and sat next to him. "He died, Rosa. He died right there in front of me," he said quietly. Rosa had never seen Rego so spooked before. She knew he wasn't making it up.

"What's in the case? What's it for?" she asked.

"I don't know. He told me all these crazy things before he died." Rego stood up and paced around the floor. "He said I should never open it."

"Oh c'mon. Let me see this thing, we've got to see what's in it at least," she said as she picked up the satchel. "We need to take it and hand it over to the police. You need to tell them you didn't do anything," Rosa insisted.

"No, I don't think so," he said quickly and took the satchel out of her hands and put it back on the desk. "That's the last thing I want to do. You don't understand. *He knew who I was*."

"He did? Who was he?" she asked. Her curiosity and concern were quickly growing.

"I have no idea," he said helplessly. "He didn't tell me his name, but he sure knew who I was. He knew my name and he told me very specific things. And, he said I was the one who should do them. Oh Rosa, I'm going crazy here!" His mind was aching.

"Calm down, Rego," she said softly. "Come here, sit down. What did he tell you that you should do?"

Rego sat next to her and stared at the floor. "It didn't make any sense, Rosie. He told me to take the case and bring it to the Sister of St. Paul at Mdina."

"Mdina? What's that?" she thought out loud.

"I have no idea! I don't know what or where it is. But, he said it twice and said I must go there with the case." He sat up and shook his head and started to come back down to Earth. "I didn't even know St. Paul had a sister."

Rosa laughed and was glad to see him calming down. She put her arm around him. "We'll figure this out, Rego. Don't worry. You need to rest now." They sat against the headboard of his bed and propped their feet up on the bed. They both just sat and stared at the leather satchel across the room.

Chapter 3

Rego woke up early the next morning. He walked out into the hallway to check on his grandmother. She wasn't in her chair, so he felt relieved that she had gone to bed. He grabbed some bread from the cupboard and ate it as he stared out the window. Then he heard a commotion down on the street and he quickly realized what must be going on.

He quickly threw on some clothes and went down to the street and tried to blend in with a gathering crowd on the corner. Two police cars were parked on the street and an ambulance was near the alley. He peered around the corner to see two paramedics putting the body of Jacomé on a stretcher, his face covered over. Rego looked all around feeling paranoid and scared. He tried not to look suspicious.

A block away, Coutier stood looking on at the scene. He observed everyone on the street, where they lived, how they reacted. He didn't know any of their faces, but he did have a name. He just needed to wait for the street to calm down and clear before he could start searching the names on all the door ringers. *It would be easy*, he thought.

Rego went back inside and decided not to tell his grandmother about the satchel. He stowed it away in his closet where he knew she wouldn't see it. *I have to make sense of all this*, he thought. "I have to find out what the old man meant."

His grandmother was back in her easy chair with her eyes closed. He walked alongside the chair and put his hand on her shoulder. "I'll be back, Grandma." Then he turned and walked out of the apartment.

Rego walked to the staircase of Rosa's building and rang the buzzer for her door. A window opened three floors up and a head poked out of it. "I'll be down in a minute!" Rosa shouted as

22

she ducked back inside. Rego walked to the bottom of the steps and sat on the last one.

He watched as the cars and pedestrians passed by. He kept thinking of what happened the night before. *Why was the man shot? How did the man know him?* He was eager to piece all the clues together. He thought about all the people that passed by, totally unaware of what he was going through. Rego wished he was just like the people passing by, with nothing like this to worry about. All he wanted to do was go to school and play football.

A few minutes later, Rosa came out of the apartment building and sat next to him on the doorsteps. "So, what do we do first?" she asked.

"I have to find out what the old man meant, last night," Rego responded. "But I have no idea how to find this Mdina place. And the Sister of St. Paul, I have no clue." He threw his hands up.

"You know why you don't know where to look for Mdina?" she asked wryly. "Because you have to go somewhere you have never been to." Rego looked at her as if she were crazy. She lightly slapped the top of his forehead with her hand. "The library at school! Come on."

They both jumped up and headed towards their school that was a few blocks away. "OK, but no more hitting me," Rego said with a grin.

Back in Rego's neighborhood, the street activity was back to normal and the crowd had left the scene where the body was found. Coutier casually walked from door to door, looking at all the names on the door ringers at each entry.

He finally came to the door of the building where Rego and his grandmother lived. He looked down the list of names and then saw the one he was looking for, Ouliveyra. It was next to apartment number 3A. He decided not to ring the buzzer and stepped down the stairs and stood on the street. He lit a cigarette and waited.

Soon a woman walked out of the door and passed Coutier without even looking at him. He watched her walk away, and then quickly jumped up the stairs to catch the door before it closed. He flicked his cigarette to the ground and stepped on it, discarding it on the floor in the hallway. He looked up the stairwell to see them winding its way to the top. He made his way to the third floor and walked to the door with a 3A painted on the outside. He raised his hand to knock on the door, but then he stopped his fist in mid-air.

The hell with this, he thought. *I don't need to knock for this old bird.* He pulled a small metal pick from his overcoat and began to slide it into the door latch to pick it.

"What the hell are you doing?" demanded a voice behind him. Coutier slipped his hand in his coat pockets and turned around with a smile. Behind him stood Mr. Vittierri, the building superintendent. He lived right across the hallway in apartment 3B.

"Ah, good morning, sir. How are you this fine day?" Coutier said coyly.

"I said what are you doing to that door? What the hell are you trying to do, break in or something?" Mr. Vittierri demanded again.

"Of course not, sir. I merely wanted to speak to the lady of the house. I knocked on the door with my ink pen, that is all."

"I don't believe that for a second!" Mr. Vittierri said. He was no fool. "You leave that poor woman alone! This is my building and I don't want anybody bothering my tenants. And I don't want to see nobody selling in here either! Now get the hell out!"

Coutier tipped his hat and slowly walked down the stairwell to the entry door. Mr. Vittierri watched him intently as he walked all the way down. Coutier reached the bottom and then heard a voice shout down at him, "And don't let me catch you in here again, you hear?" Coutier looked at him with a frown on his face, and then he walked out.

Rego and Rosa sat at a long table in the college library where they attended. "So, this is what the library looks like on the inside," Rego said sarcastically.

Rosa ignored him and flipped through a stack of encyclopedias. She opened the book labeled M and thumbed her way through to the Me section and saw nothing. She thought for a moment and looked at Rego. "You are sure he said, '*M-dina*', right? Not M*e*dina?"

"Nope," Rego said staring at her legs. "I'm sure he said Mdina." She turned her legs away from him and flipped a few more pages in the book.

"Here it is. I found it!" she said with excitement. She read out loud to him, "*Mdina – The ancient medieval town on the island of Malta. It is the old capital of Malta and has remnants that date back to the year 4000 B.C. It is known as the 'Silent City' and has a commanding view of the entire island.*" She smiled at him in triumph.

Rego looked at her puzzled. "The island of Malta? Where the hell is that? Please tell me it is off the coast of Brazil."

Rosa quickly flipped the pages back in the same book and found the name Malta. "Nope," she said still staring at the book.

"Well, is it *near* Brazil?" he asked hopefully.

"Not *quite*," she said sliding the book in front of him. Rego looked down at the encyclopedia entry and saw that it had a small map showing the location of Malta. In the center of the Mediterranean Sea, directly between Sicily and North Africa, was a tiny circle with a star in the center with the name 'Malta' next to it. Underneath the name was another name in smaller letters that read, 'Valletta'.

"Off the coast of North Africa. Just perfect," Rego said with disgust. "You can't even see the place. It's so tiny on this map. It's just a speck on the map."

Rosa pulled the book away from him again. She became more and more intrigued with the tiny island. "Valletta must be the capital city now. It said Mdina was the ancient capital, so that's why it says Valletta by the star." She started to read about the island itself and looked at the map some more. "Wow! That is a long way off."

"Tell me about it," Rego said with his head down on the table.

"I wonder what it is like there." Rosa was fascinated. "Hey, they speak English." She read the passage further. "And Maltese too."

"Great, neither one does me any good," Rego complained. Rego was clearly discouraged. A look of despair and loss of hope came over him. "Can we go now?" He pulled himself out of his chair and stood behind her. She looked at him and remembered the reality of the situation again. She nodded and got up from the table.

They sat outside the library on the steps. Rego had his forehead resting in his palm, and he sat shaking his head back and forth. "What am I going to do, Rosa? This is too much. If the man really meant this island, then it is impossible. How would I get there? I've hardly been twenty kilometers outside of Brasilia, much less out of the country." His mind was racing again and was clearly distraught about what he had to do. "I just can't do this."

Rosa sat thinking, occasionally looking over at Rego, then back at the people walking by in front of them. "There must be a way," she thought out loud.

"It's no use, Rosie," Rego said, throwing up his hands. "This place must be halfway around the world." He shook his head in panic and thought of an alternative she had suggested the night before. "Maybe you're right. Maybe I should just take it to the police. I did nothing wrong. I got nothing to worry about, right?"

Rosa grabbed his hand from the air and looked directly at him. "What about the man on the street? You can't just ignore what he asked you to do. You told me that he died right in front of you. Don't you remember? He was obviously intending to find you and talk to you some more about this request. He just didn't count on being shot before he had the chance. Think about what this must have meant to that poor man."

"I know, I know," he said sorely. "But let's look at the other facts. I can't fly there, it would cost way too much. I can't even afford to go on a ship. I don't think I could find much more than a couple hundred cruzeiros. That won't get me very far."

Then a light went off in Rosa's head. "Maybe you *could* go by ship, Rego. You could take a bus down to Rio or Sao Paulo, or even to Salvador. There are ports at all those cities. My brother works at the bus depot. I bet he could find a way to get you on one of those buses."

"And when I get to the port, then what?" he asked. "How do I find a ship to Malta, and how do I pay for it?"

"You get a job, silly," she said smiling brilliantly. "You *can* work on those ships. That way they pay you and then you can find your way to the Mediterranean."

"Find me way? he asked incredulously. "Ah, you make it sound so easy. And besides, it may take weeks or months to finally make it. I don't want to be away from here that long, away from you." Then he remembered something else. "And what about Grandma? I can't leave her, Rosa. I have to look after her."

"Away from me? I need to get you out of my hair for a while anyway," she said with a shy grin. Her face grew serious at that moment. "I will look after Grandma, you know that. But the more I think about that satchel and how that man died for it, the more I think that you really need to do this." Rosa knew she didn't want him to leave. She couldn't imagine how frightened he must feel knowing such a tremendous task faced him.

Rego thought a little more, and then put his hand into Rosa's. "Do you really think he meant this island when he said Mdina? Do you really think that is the place?" She nodded with confidence as she grasped his hand tight. He took a deep breath and looked in her eyes. "You have the prettiest eyes. And, you always know what to say." Then he nodded in acceptance. "You are right. I will do it."

Chapter 4

Night came, and the cool winds were blowing through the streets. Rego had walked Rosa home and he wandered for a while thinking about the task ahead.

He came upon the neighborhood cathedral, Santo Marco, and he stopped in front of the steps by the front door. His grandmother attended Mass regularly before his grandfather died, but her health deteriorated rapidly after that. As the years passed, the other parishioners noticed her less and less at Mass. Since she stopped going, Rego started to skip Mass as well. She encouraged him to go, but when he left for Mass, he just skipped the other way down the street towards the playing fields and ended up playing football all Sunday long. Long before his grandfather passed away, however, he used to attend Mass with his grandparents every Sunday. He even became an altar boy.

Rego stood in front of the door to Santo Marco's and stared at the door handle. Slowly, he opened the large door and walked in. He dipped the tips of his fingers in the holy water basin and made the sign of the cross, looking at the large altar way down in front. He walked slowly up the aisle and sat at the end of a pew in the middle of the cathedral. He looked at the high vaulted ceilings, decorated very ornately. The familiar stain glass windows lined the sides of the church and the same crucifix hung high above behind the altar. He saw the door to the Sacristy where he always had to go to don the altar boy's cassock before Mass. He gazed at the large candle holders that lined the main altar, the same ones he would light before Mass started.

He sat for a while just looking straight ahead. He wondered what it would be like traveling by sea. He had never been on a ship before. He had never been to Rio de Janeiro or Sao Paulo. Once he had been to Salvador when he was six, right after the terrible murder of his parents. His grandfather thought it would be good for him to get out of the big city for a while and help him adjust to the loss of his parents. He tried to remember being there but only had scant memories of his time there.

All he remembered was his Uncle Enso loved to give him coins. Each time he saw him, Uncle Enso would say, "Rego, do you have something behind your ear?" Or he would say, "Rego do you have something up your sleeve?" Each time Enso would put his hand to Rego's ear, or his shirt sleeve, and quickly produce a shiny coin. "Here, it's a good thing I caught it. You almost lost it!" He gave Rego the coin every time and Rego would smile and give him a hug. By the time he returned to Brasilia, he had a whole pouch full of coins.

Rego pulled the kneeler down and leaned forward to kneel on it. He leaned over the pew in front of him and began to pray silently, "Lord, I know I haven't come to see you lately. I'm sorry about that. But you give us the nice sun on Sundays, so it is hard to not go to the fields and play football." He thought for a few moments more. "Lord, I had forgotten how beautiful your house is inside. I didn't know I missed it so much. I will come more often, I promise." He lowered his head and became frightened. "Lord, I have to go away, and I am very scared. I don't know why this task has been given to me, but I feel I must go and do it. Watch over Grandma and Rosa, ok?" He put his head down on the back of the pew and began to sob. The responsibility began to overwhelm him. The fear of the unknown was too much to bear. He looked up at the crucifix hanging on the wall and said, "Will you watch over me, too?"

After he was done praying, he walked over to the prayer candles where many were brightly lit. He pulled a coin from his pocket and put it in the basket near the stand. He picked up an unlit candle near the top row and lit it from another burning candle. He stood for a moment, just watching it melt the fresh wax.

"Rego?" said a low voice behind him. He turned around to see his old pastor, Fr. Renaldo.

"Father, hello, how are you?" Rego said, surprised to see him. He pulled himself together and wiped his face quickly.

"I'm sorry if I startled you. I don't normally see people in here so late," responded Fr. Renaldo. "I haven't seen you in here for quite some time now."

Rego felt ashamed but thought of a quick answer. "It's my grandmother. She doesn't get out much anymore and I have to keep an eye on her now."

"Are you alright, my son? You seem troubled," Fr. Renaldo said, concerned. "I'd be happy to talk to you about whatever is on your mind."

"No, that's ok. I just wanted to light a candle. You know, not having been here in so long," Rego said looking back towards the candles. "I had better be going now, Father. It was nice seeing you again."

"Of course, Rego. Hopefully I will see you at Mass," he said with a smile.

Rego started to walk down the aisle towards the door. Then he turned around and said to the pastor who was still standing by the candles, "Father, have you ever been on a journey and when you got there, you didn't find what you were looking for?"

"All of us have a journey in life," he answered. "All journeys are not without a purpose, though. You may not find something in the end, but something always finds you."

Rego thought for a moment on what he meant, but he did not understand. "Thanks Father, I'll remember that. I better get home."

"Good night, Rego," Fr. Renaldo called out to him.

Rego unlocked the door to his apartment when Mr. Vittierri stuck his head out of the door across the hall.

"Hey Rego, is that you?"

"Sorry, Mr. Vittierri, am I making too much noise?" Rego asked.

"Now that you mention it, yes you are," he said sarcastically. "But, that's not why I came out here. I caught some nutcase in an overcoat messing around with your door today. But I ran his ass off and told him not to come here again."

Rego remembered the man from last night that stood over the dead man in the alley. *How did he find me so quickly?* he thought. *Did he see me last night?* He looked at Mr. Vittierri and asked, "Did he say why he was here?"

"I don't know, I thought he was trying to mess with the lock, but he said he just wanted to talk to your grandma," Mr. Vittierri said. "I thought he was full of it, so I told him to beat it. I don't want any rotten salesman in here. I just thought I'd let you know. Good night, kid." He quickly shut the door.

Rego went inside to see his grandmother asleep in front of the TV again. He touched her on the shoulder and said, "I'm home Grandma." She twitched her head a little to the side but didn't open her eyes.

He sat in his room, thinking of what he should take with him. He decided he should take as little as possible. He stared at the satchel now sitting on his desk again. Over on the mirror, stuck to the side, was a football card with a picture of Pelé. He wore a yellow and blue uniform, dribbling the ball down the pitch. It was the only trading card he had of his favorite player. He took the picture down and slid it into his coat pocket along with his identification papers. The first match of the World Cup wasn't until the first week of June, nearly two weeks away. He wondered where he would be then.

All he packed was his jacket and a comb and toothbrush. He stuffed them into one coat pocket and a clean shirt in the other. He knew it may get cold at night on the ships.

He could hardly sleep at all. The strange man in the overcoat obviously knew where he was now, and he was after the case.

So, he had no choice but to leave now. Plus, he didn't want to put his grandmother in danger. He lay in bed and stared at the ceiling and thought about what Fr. Renaldo had said. *What if I get there and it is all for nothing?* he thought to himself. He closed his eyes and tried to sleep but sleep escaped him most of the night.

Early the next morning, Rego was up and ready to go. He had only slept a few hours but was full of adrenaline and energy. It was still dark outside on this early Saturday morning.

He quickly made some extra sandwiches in the kitchen and stuffed them into a brown paper bag and put them in the inside pocket of his jacket. He nervously walked into the den where his grandmother had slept all night in her chair. He quietly walked over to the TV and switched it off. Then he knelt beside his grandmother and put his hand on hers.

"I'm sorry, Grandma, but I have to go now," he said sadly. "And, I don't know how long I will be gone. But, I promise I will be back as soon as I can. I promise." He looked at her pale face with her eyes closed, then he looked at the floor. He gazed at her one last time, then stood and grabbed his coat and the leather satchel and quietly walked out of the apartment. As soon as the door shut, his grandmother lifted her eyes open with sadness.

Coutier stood behind a corner in the darkness. He watched as Rego stepped lightly down the stairs and walked briskly down the street. The satchel was flung over his shoulder. *I knew it,* he thought to himself, and began to follow him.

Rego's grandmother stood in the doorway of his bedroom. A wrinkled frown was pasted to her expression as she panned over the room. She stood in her rumpled nightgown with her hands folded together in front of her. Her eyes were red from lack of sleep.

She looked at the mirror that once held Rego's trading card with a picture of Pelé on it. She knew of only one reason why Rego had left. She stared in silence with a look of sadness and loss. She shook her head and said quietly to herself, "Enso."

The sun had started to rise by the time Rego reached Rosa's building. She was already waiting for him on the stairs. Rosa looked as if she had not slept much either.

It was one of those typical Saturday mornings in Brasilia. The traffic on the streets bustled. Pedestrians walking everywhere, people on bicycles riding all around. People were out running their errands before the work week began again.

They waited at the bus stop to catch the main terminal bus back to the station. Rosa was quiet, sitting on the bench, not looking up from the ground as they waited. Rego looked at her every couple of minutes but she never looked at him.

"He will be waiting for us at the station, right?" he asked in hopes she would talk to him, or at least look at him.

"Yes," she said softly, still staring at the ground.

Rego stared ahead of him and never said anything more until the bus arrived. They both sat together near the front of the bus.

Then, Rosa finally broke the silence. "I made you some biscuits for lunch. I even put butter on them," she said, handing him a brown paper bag. She placed it on his lap and laid her hand on top of his and just stared at their hands. She looked at him and wrinkled her nose and cleared her throat. "Don't eat them all at once like a pig!" She pulled her hand away and turned to look straight ahead again.

Rego smiled at her. *What would I do without her?* he thought. "I won't eat them all at once. Thanks Rosie," he said and leaned over and kissed her cheek.

"Hey, stop it, I just put makeup on," she said, pushing his face back. Rego just sat and smiled at her. He loved her spirit.

They arrived at the bus station to a scene of marketplace chaos. People were everywhere. For on Saturdays there were always open-air markets with fresh vegetables and fruits. The shopkeepers knew to set up near the bus station for people to buy food to take on weekend trips and getaways. It was a common sight on a Saturdays. Amidst the throng of buyers and sellers were the buses lined up in their assigned spots. The buses were different sizes but were all painted white and light green. Each one had a sign in the front window and another on the side window, near the door, specifying their next destination. Rio de Janeiro, Sáo Paulo, Vitória, Cuiaba, Sáo Luis, Salvador, Aracaju, Fortaleza, and even Porto Alegre. Those were just some of the buses going to towns and cities around the country. There were also rows of buses heading for faraway cities outside of Brazil, such as Buenos Aires, Asunción, Larstown, Caracas, La Paz, and Lima. These buses were painted in the same fashion but also had a thin yellow stripe running across the top to signify it was an international bus.

This was the center of activity in Brasilia and Saturday was the busiest day of the week. Besides the routes heading out of the city, there was also the local section of bus changes. The bus from southern Brasilia pulled into the crowded station and passengers began to file off. Rosa and Rego walked together in the middle of the throng.

Coutier was never far behind keeping out of their sight. He soon met up with two other men dressed in the same overcoats and wearing the same dark brown fedoras. Their names were Gomes and LaBonne. Coutier motioned to them to look towards the ticket queue for Rio de Janeiro.

"There he is," he said to Gomes and LaBonne. "See the coat?" They both could see the satchel under Rego's arm and his jacket thrown over it. "Don't lose sight of him. Wait for my signal then we will close in on him."

Gomes and LaBonne went in different directions to try and surround them. They walked slowly ducking in and around the hordes of people. They kept within sight of Coutier as well and awaited his signal.

Rego and Rosa stood far back in a long line for the ticket booth. There was no telling what time he could get a ticket for the next bus to Rio. He looked around impatiently and nervously. He stood high on his toes to look ahead of the line. "Why is it moving so slow?" he muttered to himself. Then he spotted something familiar. Across the tops of all the people around him, he could see a familiar, dark hat slowly walking towards the front of the line. He looked to the right and saw another man wearing the same hat. He strained as hard as he could to see over all the people to see who was wearing the hat. Rosa looked at him curiously. Rego turned around to look behind him, and then he saw him. Rego and Coutier's eyes locked on one another. Coutier stared at him like a lion stares down its prey. Rego gently took Rosa by the arm and whispered to her, "It's time."

Rosa looked at Rego with a determined yet concerned look. "Ok, follow me, quickly." She grabbed his hand and led him through the crowd. She headed for the main terminal building, then turned and headed towards the marketplace. Coutier strained to see where they were going. He motioned to Gomes, then to LaBonne, and pointed towards the market and gave them the signal to follow Rosa and Rego. He tried to track them as well, weaving his way through the crowd, pushing people aside. Rosa ducked to one side of the market and then made her way to a small building between the market and the terminal. Her brother, Joao, stood near a small doorway that read "No Entry" that faced the back side of the building. Joao became alert when he spotted her.

"In here, fast!" he said to her and Rego. They ran behind the small building and went inside and shut the door behind them. It was a small maintenance room with brooms and mops and various cleaning tools. Joao was employed at the station as part of the cleaning crew. "We must hurry. These are my friends to help us, just as you asked." Three other young boys stood inside the room, dressed very similarly to Rego. They were friends of his from the football fields in the neighborhoods, Martin, Diego and Jorge.

"Thank you for coming, my friends. Nice shirts," he said with a sly smile. "Ready to have some fun with these guys?"

They all smiled at him and held up bundles under their arms, and all had jackets thrown over them. Joao handed Rego a bus pass. "This ticket is good for any of the buses, so pick a good one," he said, handing Rego a piece of paper.

Rego thanked Joao and said, "You are a good man. I owe you one." He shook his hand and said, "Take care of your sister, ok? She makes the best biscuits." Joao nodded with a smile.

He looked at Rosa, "I guess this is it, pretty eyes. Wish me luck." She grabbed his hand gave it a hard squeeze.

"Just come back, alright?" she said as she stood close to him. She looked at her brother and then decided she didn't care if he told their parents. She kissed Rego's lips quickly and passionately. "And don't screw this up, you hear me? Now get out of here." Rego gazed at her lovingly one last time and then looked at his accomplices.

"Let's go boys," he said quietly.

They all slipped one by one out of the maintenance room and blended into the crowds of people. All except Rego, who waited behind the building. Martin slowly headed to the line for Rio, Diego went to the line for Sao Paulo and Jorge casually walked over to the line for Salvador. They stood far away from one another trying to stay out of sight. The three men with the dark brown hats marched through the crowds, scouring over everything. Coutier went one way, Gomes another, and LaBonne a third way. They spread out, combing through the queues.

Suddenly, Gomes spotted him, standing far up in the queue holding the satchel and jacket under his arms. He smiled and quickly pushed his way towards Rego. Meanwhile, LaBonne spotted Rego standing in another line. At the same time, Coutier caught a glimpse of Rego in another. Each agent pushed and shoved his way to the front where Rego huddled over near the ticket booth.

Coutier strode up behind Rego and with a look of victory, grabbed his arm and spun him around. "Brazilian government. Don't move!" He yanked the jacket away from his arms and a bundle of fresh mangos fell to the ground. Coutier looked in surprise to see it wasn't Rego.

"Hey, that was my lunch!" protested Martin. "What's the matter with you?"

"Damnit!" shouted Coutier. He threw the jacket to the ground in disgust and ran off.

Gomes grabbed Rego's arm and said in a stern voice, "Don't move, I am with the Brazilian government!" He pulled the jacket away and three papayas fell to the ground.

"My papayas! Look what you've done." shouted Diego. Gomes' eyes grew wide when he saw it was not Rego and slammed the jacket to the ground. "Hey, what do you have against my jacket?" Diego yelled to Gomes as he darted away. He laughed out loud as the agent cursed as he ran.

"Freeze! Brazilian government! You're coming with me!" LaBonne barked to another fake Rego. Jorge lifted his arms in surrender and the jacket filled with oranges and apples fell to the ground. LaBonne looked at him in dismay. "It's not him. Damn!" He ran into the crowd, looking frantically for the real Rego.

Jorge shouted back at him, "Hey, I thought you were hungry!" He took a bite from one the apples and smiled as the agent stumbled away.

Rego ran as fast as he could to the foreign terminal and found the shortest line he could see for buses about to depart. He jumped on the bus, not even noticing where it was going, and hurried down the aisle and sat near the back on the left side. He tried to get as far from sight as possible. His heart pounded as he crouched in his seat and waited for the engine to start. The bus was crowded as all manner of people boarded the bus. Finally, the doors were closed and the engine roared to life.

The bus slowly began to pull away and Rego remained huddled low in his seat. An old woman took her seat next to him as the bus began to speed up. He gingerly sat up as she looked at him crazily with his head held below the window. "I think we're off the ground now, son," she said laughing to herself. He sat up and smiled sarcastically at her.

Back at the terminal, Coutier, Gomes and LaBonne found each other among the hordes of people. They were not amused and could not see Rego anywhere. They spun around, looking in all directions fruitlessly. Coutier gritted his teeth and stormed off towards the terminal.

Rosa sat on a bench nearby and stared in the direction of the buses pulled away into the streets. Joao sat next to her, looking hopefully in the same direction. Soon they were joined by the three impersonators, Martin, Diego, and Jorge. They all congratulated each other on the success of their ruse. However, Rosa did not smile. Her expression never even changed. She just sat there with a simple look of pale sadness. As she watched the buses pull away, one by one, a single tear rolled down her cheek.

Rego situated himself on the bus and put the satchel down on the floor between his knees. He began to look around the bus at all the people riding with him. Almost all of them had traveling bags or large purses with them, obviously settling in for a long journey.

He turned towards the old woman next to him and asked, "Where is this bus going, anyway?"

Once again, she looked at him as if he were crazy. "Where do *you* think this bus is going?" she asked with sarcasm.

"I was hoping I jumped on the bus going to Caracas," he said anticipating the right response. The old woman laughed heartily at him for what seemed an eternity.

"I hope not, young man. I may be almost blind, but when I got on, the sign said La Paz," she said still laughing.

Rego rolled his eyes and buried his head in his hands. He glanced at the woman with bewilderment and asked, "La Paz, Bolivia?" She nodded her head yes, still chuckling to herself. "Ah crap, that's just perfect. How long does it take to get there?"

"Not as long as it used to," she answered without hesitating. "It's only about thirty hours, plus a change of driver at the border."

Rego sat in his seat with a numbed expression. He had run so fast, he had jumped on the closest bus he could find. He shook his head at his luck. *At least it wasn't going to Argentina,* he thought. The bus pulled over on the outskirts of the city to do a ticket check. The driver went down the aisle slowly checking each passenger's ticket. Rego handed him the pass Joao had given him. The driver looked at it and quietly moved on. When he reached the back of the bus, the driver turned to head back to the front seat. Rego stood partially up when he came by his seat and asked him, "Excuse me, sir? Does it really take thirty hours to get to La Paz?"

"No, of course not. Don't be silly," he said. Rego's expression turned hopeful when he heard that. "It's only about twenty-eight." The driver casually walked back to the front and started the bus in motion once again.

Rego remained standing, staring ahead in disgust. He slumped back into his seat and mumbled to himself, "Shit."

Chapter 5

"I want a list of every bus that departed out of the city, between ten and ten-thirty this morning," Coutier demanded inside the terminal office. He was beside himself that Rego had gotten away from all three of them. Gomes and LaBonne stood nearby looking ridiculous.

"Yes, sir, I will get you the list right away," the terminal manager said and began flipping through his log books. Within minutes he produced a list of routes for the agents. "I have it here, sir. We had six buses leave in that time. We had two leave for São Paulo, and one each left for Asunción, Curitiba, La Paz and Belém."

Coutier studied the list carefully. "LaBonne, send two men to São Paulo and meet the buses there. Send two more to Asunción and Curitiba. I will go to Belém. That is the nearest port that I think he will go. He wants to get out of here as fast as he can. You two morons go to La Paz. Better yet, get to the border crossing before the bus does. Tell your men to do the same for the bus to Asunción. If you see Rego, report to me at once! Hold him until I get there." He rolled up the list and held it in his fist and pointed it at LaBonne, "No more screw ups this time!"

The bus traveled slowly westward throughout the day. It only stopped for refueling and rest stops for the passengers. It rolled on through the night. Rego could hardly keep his eyes open since he slept so little the night before, but as soon as fell asleep, the bumps in the road would jar him awake. As he stared into the darkness, he could see a light starting to illuminate the sky. It was nearing daybreak, and the bus was getting closer to the border crossing.

The sun came over the horizon when the bus rolled up to the border crossing. The stop was also a place to change drivers and give the passengers a chance to rest and stretch their legs. Rego stood outside the bus, yawning and stretching. He took out some of the biscuits Rosa had made for him and ate one. He had one more sandwich for lunch that hopefully would hold him over until they reached La Paz.

He noticed a small car with the top down parked beside the border office. Rego thought it was a very sporty car, but he noticed it had a government tag on the back. He looked at the satchel hanging around his shoulder. He decided not to take any more chances by standing out in the open and climbed back on the bus. He would have to wait another twenty to thirty minutes before the bus would leave again. He sat low in the seat, keeping an eye on the small convertible, waiting to see if anyone came out to it.

The old woman slowly made her way back down the aisle of the bus and sat down. "You sure like to sit on this bus. Don't you want to get out and stretch your legs a bit?" she asked him.

"I did, I did," he said innocently. "I'm just ready to get back on the road, is all." He looked back out the window and stared at the car. Just then, two men wearing the fedoras walked out of the border office and walked over to the car. Rego grew nervous and impatient. He recognized them from the bus station in Brasilia. Rego jumped up and started to get off the bus. "You're right. I better go to the bathroom before we leave," Rego said hurrying off the bus.

He watched from inside the men's room door as LaBonne and Gomes walked over to the bus. They got on and started walking up and down the aisle. After they did not find Rego, they stepped off and a new bus driver climbed aboard and shut the door. Rego waited for their backs to turn as they walked away from the bus, then he made a dash for the bus door. He tapped on the glass frantically, holding up his ticket, waiting for the driver to open the door.

The door opened finally, "Come on, kid, I don't have all day," the driver groaned. Rego jumped on the bus and ducked down low as he skirted down the aisle. He slid into his seat, crawling over the old woman. The bus engine roared to life as he crouched down in his seat to hide his face.

The old woman looked at him with a perplexed look again, "Almost time for takeoff again, eh kid?" she asked with a laugh.

"Um, yes. I hate this part," Rego answered going along with her. He looked anxiously to the front of the bus as the driver finally put the bus into gear. "Come on, come on," Rego muttered under his breath. The bus slowly pulled away and passed through the gate into Bolivia.

As the bus passed the government car, Gomes glanced up and caught a glimpse of a face he recognized. He shouted to LaBonne, "The kid! I think I saw the kid! He must have been hiding."

"Are you sure?" LaBonne said in astonishment. "We searched that whole damn bus!"

"I'm not for certain, but I think that was the little punk's face," Gomes insisted again. They both ran for their car and jumped in. The gate lifted for them as they sped past into Bolivia.

As the bus started to speed up, Rego relaxed a little in his seat. He thought he had given the two agents the slip. They were getting near to La Paz but the drive would become slower as they started to climb into the Andes Mountains. The roads became more and more windy and the hills grew higher and steeper.

Rego let out a heavy sigh and put his head back. Out of the corner of his eye, he saw a small car pulling up alongside the bus. Startled, he sat up in his seat and peered outside his window. *Shit. It's the agents!* he thought to himself.

Gomes started pointing towards Rego's window. The car came alongside the driver and motioned for him to pull over.

The driver looked agitated and ignored them. Rego watched as they pulled closer, waving frantically at the driver, but he continued to ignore them.

They can't do anything to me here, we're in Bolivia now, Rego thought. Just then, LaBonne swerved the car over and banged it into the side of the bus. Everyone started screaming on the bus as it began swerving all over the road. The bus driver struggled as he kept it on the road as they raced over the top of a hill. Rego climbed over the old woman and leapt over bags amidst the screaming people, trying to get to the driver.

LaBonne rammed the side of the bus again, prompting more screams and chaos. Rego stumbled his way to the driver, "Go faster, man! Go faster, you can outrun this guy," Rego pleaded with the driver.

"Get out of here, kid. I can't control this thing!" the driver yelled back.

"*No.* You have to knock this asshole off the road. Go faster!" Rego exclaimed.

In the chaos, a few old women behind the driver started whopping Rego on the head with their purses and yelling at him, "Sit down. Sit down, you stupid kid!"

Rego swatted he purses away, wincing in pain. He persisted though. "Get this damn thing moving. Cut him off, cut him off!"

The old women kept banging him on the head and the bus driver struggled with the bus to keep it on the road as they barreled down the hill. All of the sudden, a gunshot rang out from the car. Everybody screamed even more. The bus driver fell over on his side, holding his arm, moaning in agony. The bus started to veer out of control.

Rego scrambled to his feet, as the purses stopped flying at his head. He saw Gomes pointing the gun again, this time at the tires. Rego pulled and strained to get the injured driver out of his seat and then jumped behind the wheel, struggling with all his might to pull it back under control. He slammed his foot on the

44

brakes and swerved to the left sharply and smashed into the side of the car. Gomes dropped the gun and before he could react, LaBonne lost control and ran off the road, slamming into a tree. Rego pulled hard to the right and finally straightened the bus and slowing it down. He kept it rolling though and cheers rang out from the passengers. Rego felt the knot on his head and winced in pain from all the purses that had bombarded his head.

He looked at the driver on the floor holding his arm. "Are you alright, sir?" he asked.

"The bastards shot me," the man wailed, still stunned from what happened.

Rego yelled over his shoulder, "Someone help him to a seat, his arm is bleeding badly. We'll get you to a doctor, sir, don't you worry." An older man stood and helped the driver get into the front seat on the right side of the bus. Some women bandaged his arm and gave him some water to drink. The people continued clapping as Rego drove the bus as fast as he could towards the mountains.

Two hours later, Rego topped one last hill and then saw the city before them. The bus limped into La Paz with very little fuel left and badly damaged.

Rego was amazed with the drive through the mountains. He had never seen them before and was astonished at the amazing sight of them. He handled the bus well on the difficult roads and as they entered the city, he was relieved. The satchel still hung across at his side with the strap across his chest. He looked at it momentarily, then stared back at the road in front of him.

He drove to an open square in the heart of the city and pulled the bus over near a large area of the square. The bus jolted to a stop and Rego shut off the engine. He stood and faced the passengers in the bus.

"Welcome to La Paz!" he announced. They all cheered and clapped for him and Rego took a bow to their applause. He saluted them one last time before stepping off the bus in triumph.

One of the old women that had pounded Rego with her purse sat next to the wounded bus driver and scolded him, "This isn't the bus station!"

Chapter 6

Rego walked down the streets of the huge city, looking for a place to sit down and find something to eat. The city was an incredible site with mountains all around. Rego marveled at the site of such wondrous nature. The snow-capped peaks looked like a postcard that surrounded the city.

The sun was bright, and the streets were active in La Paz. It was mid-day and church goers were now filing out of chapels and cathedrals after attending Mass. Rego walked down a narrow street lined with a few shops and stores. He came upon a store with the name *Manoel's* painted in red letters on the window. He decided to walk in and see if he could get something to eat.

The store was dark inside despite the bright sun outside. An overweight man with about two days growth on his beard stood behind the counter drying a beer mug. He was the owner, Manoel. He stood keeping a sharp eye on Rego as he slowly walked in. He knew he had never seen the boy before.

"What can I do for you, kid?" Manoel asked in Spanish. Rego was required to study Spanish all through school, since the rest of South America spoke Spanish and not Portuguese as they did in Brazil. So, his Spanish was not fluent, but he knew enough to carry on a conversation with someone.

Rego approached the counter, which served as a bar as well as a grocery counter. "I was wondering if you had any food to buy," he said shyly to Manoel.

"That is some accent, kid, where are you from?" Manoel asked, setting the glass down.

"Brasilia," Rego said. "Do you have any food to eat, a sandwich or something?"

"You got any money, kid?" Manoel answered, somewhat agitated.

Rego looked into his pocket to see how much he had left. "Yes, about one hundred cruzeiros." He placed the coins on the counter.

"Don't take cruzeiros, only bolivianos," Manoel said turning away.

"Are you sure? This is all I have, sir," Rego pleaded with a hint of desperation.

"What do I look like, kid, a bank?" Manoel retorted as he reached to clean more glasses. "Can't take no cruzeiros. Go see if you can exchange them at the bank down the street."

"Today is Sunday, sir," Rego responded with growing disappointment. "I am sure the bank is closed."

"Sorry, kid." Manoel looked Rego over and could see he must have just come into the city and had no means to buy anything. "What's your name, kid?"

"Rego Ouliveyra, sir."

"Call me Manny. I tell you what, take some of that jerky in that jar, it's getting old anyway." Rego nodded with an eager smile and grabbed a couple sticks of jerky. He quickly began to devour them. "How long have you been in La Paz?" he asked.

"About an hour," Rego said with a mouthful of jerky. "I just came in on the bus. Well, I drove the bus, actually," Rego said, now remembering what he had just gone through.

"A bus driver, huh? Where's your bus then?" Manny asked sarcastically.

"Oh, it's not my bus. I took over the driving after the driver got shot," Rego said casually.

Manny set his glass down and looked at Rego with a perplexed expression. "You're fooling me, kid."

"Nope."

"Ha!" Manny laughed, slapping his hand down on the counter. "That's a good one, kid. I'll have to remember that one." He walked further down the counter still laughing to himself.

Rego took another bite of the jerky, then yelled down the counter, "Do you think the bank will give me much for these coins, Manny?"

"I doubt it. Ain't worth much around here," Manny said matter-of-factly.

Rego frowned. He noticed a dusty TV set sitting on the counter behind the bar. "Hey, are you going to watch the World Cup?"

"Is Bolivia competing in it?" Manny asked without looking back at Rego.

Rego thought for a moment. "I don't think so."

"Then I could care less about that shit," Manny said with contempt.

"Not me, I hope I get to see some of it. Pelé is my favorite player," Rego said with a smile. He took another bite of his jerky.

Manny ignored him. Football was the last thing he wanted to discuss. He hated the game.

"Do you think I could have a job here working for you, Manny?" Rego blurted out of the blue.

Manny turned way around and looked at Rego with bewilderment. "A job? Here? Can't do it, kid. Ain't got enough work here for me as it is." Manny began to grow tired of Rego. "You better finish up there, kid, I've got work to do."

Rego sat quietly, finishing the last piece of beef jerky. Now he was thirsty, but he didn't have the nerve to ask Manny for something to drink. He could tell his welcome was quickly wearing thin. He looked around thinking what he could do next. He needed to find a way to get some money, so he could take another bus to Lima. That was the next logical place for him to find a ship.

"Damnit," Rego said out loud. He made sure Manny heard him.

"What the hell is it now, kid?" Manny asked frowning at Rego.

"My head is killing me, ever since we started up those mountains," Rego said. He really did have a bad headache.

Manny laughed again. "It's the mountain air, kid. Up here is God's country. Up here, you are on top of the world! We see all from here. That is the pride of La Paz. But since we are so high in the sky, the air ain't as thick as it is where you come from. That's why your head hurts. You'll get used to it. Here, drink some of this water."

Rego had a feeling it was the high altitude of the city. He saw the elevation sign when he drove in on the bus. The city rested higher than 3300 meters. Rego smiled when Manny handed him some water to drink. He knew his headache might come in handy.

The door opened to the store and a man walked in and passed Rego, not even noticing him. He walked down the counter to where Manny was sifting through some boxes.

"What do you say, Manny?" the man asked the bartender.

"Alonso, come on in my friend," Manny said with a smile. The men shook hands. "How are the fields coming along?"

"Slow. And, too much damn dust out there. I need a pint to clear out my throat," Alonso said pointing to the beer tap. Manny obliged and drew some beer into a mug for him.

Alonso owned a small potato farm on the outskirts of the city and ran it with his brother Miguel. The crops grew smaller each year, though, as the rains fell less and less. He took a long drink from his mug of beer and wiped his mouth with his shirt sleeve. "I can't move that lazy brother of mine fast enough anymore. I don't know if I can get the sacks to market in time." He took another long drink from his mug.

"Maybe I can help you out," Manny said putting down a box on the counter. "That kid down there could probably do it for you. He was looking for work here. I told him to beat it, but he's still in here."

Alonso took another drink and drained the mug of beer, not looking down the bar. He wiped his mouth with his sleeve again, "What kid?"

Manny looked at him as if he were blind. He pointed towards Rego, saying, "That kid down at the end, the Brazilian. He'll tell you some wild stories for sure."

Alonso stared down the counter at Rego. "From Brazil, huh? What the hell is he doing here?"

"I don't know, why don't you ask him?" Manny said turning back to his work.

"Hey, kid, what's your name? Come on down here." Alonso yelled down to Rego.

Rego looked up and thought for a moment whether he should answer him. His first impression of Alonso was not a good one. He finally decided to answer him. "Rego," he said.

"Come on down here, Rego, I've got a proposition for you," Alonso said. Rego got up from his stool and walked down and sat next to Alonso.

"I'm Alonso," he said extending his hand. Rego shook his hand and stared at him.

"You just got here, eh? Where are you headed?" Alonso asked wryly.

"I'm trying to get to Lima," Rego said, trying to keep his answers short.

Alonso let out a big laugh. "You want to go to Peru? Good luck, kid. You couldn't pay me to set foot in that madhouse."

"Really, why not?" Rego asked curiously.

"Because of the revolution, that's why. Some hothead named Velasco went in there and overthrew President Belaunde a couple of years ago, and it's been chaos ever since," Alonso stated in his opinion. "I sure as hell wouldn't go there. If you do, you better tell them Velasco is the best thing since sliced bread, or they'll throw you in the clink. Or worse." Alonso took another drink from his fresh mug of beer.

Rego looked down at the counter with concern. Getting put in jail is the last thing he needed. *But where else could I go to catch a ship?* he thought. *Lima was still the best place. How bad could the revolution be after two years?*

"Manny tells me you are looking for work," Alonso interrupted Rego's deep thought. "Well, I've got some work for you, if you want it."

Rego perked up on his stool. "Oh yes, sir, I am looking for work. I need to make some money, but I don't have any place to stay."

Alonso nodded, he had it all worked out in his mind. "Well, I'm not running a boarding house, kid. I have a potato farm that my brother and I work. I need some help getting the potatoes picked and put into hauling sacks for the market. You understand, right? It's just business." Alonso thought for a moment more and looked Rego over sitting on his stool and wearing the leather satchel across his chest. "But I do have a barn you can sleep in if you want. Just have to look out for the rats," he said chuckling. Manny laughed as well.

Rego responded right away, "That sounds great to me, sir. I don't mind picking potatoes. Thank you, I will take the job."

"Good, then it is settled. Let me finish this beer and I'll take you down to the farm," Alonso said taking another long drink from his mug.

Rego rode on the back of Alonso's motorized scooter, holding a fuel can on his lap all the way to the potato farm. They pulled up a dusty road that led a half kilometer into a hilly area with a few small trees around a small wooden shack and an old barn that stood two levels. A couple of dogs ran around in a curious manner as the scooter pulled up with the two men aboard. Alonso rode the scooter to the shack and shut off the motor.

"This is it, what do you think?" he said with a beaming smile. It was paradise to Alonso. Rego didn't answer and just looked around the area in dismay. "Go take a look around the barn, pick out a spot for your things. Don't worry, there aren't any livestock in there anymore."

Rego gave him an odd look and thought the barn looked more inviting than the shack. He walked inside the barn and saw that it was almost barren. It had nothing but a dusty dirt floor and some old wooden stalls. There was an old staircase that led only halfway up the second floor. The top half of the stairs had fallen away along with the whole second level. He was amazed the barn was still standing. He looked up to see just inside the doorway, hanging from a rope, two large gunny sacks full of potatoes. The ropes extended along the wall on some rusty pulleys down to the floor where they were held in place by a pin stuck inside a round metal ring. The heavy sacks swayed back and forth very slowly making an eerie creaking sound on the rusty pulleys.

"We have to hang them up there to keep the critters and bugs out of them," an unfamiliar voice said behind him. Rego turned around to see a man wearing a dark green camouflage hat. "I am Miguel, his brother," pointing a thumb behind him towards the shack.

Rego shook his hand, "Rego Ouliveyra. Thank you for the job. I am glad to be here."

"Of course, you are," Miguel said coldly. "We will take them down tomorrow morning and load them on the mule cart. Then you will start in the fields, ok?" Rego nodded. Miguel turned and walked briskly out of the barn. Rego had the feeling Miguel was not happy to see him there, but Rego didn't much like him either.

Rego spent his days doing back-breaking work in the potato fields. The air was cool in the morning, but the wind blew swiftly on the mountain side, stirring up the dust everywhere.

He loaded the dusty potatoes into gunny sacks and dragged them to the outside of the barn.

Miguel showed him how to close the bags in a twisted knot at the top and use a vise to tighten a metal ring around the knot. Then Miguel showed him how to attach the bags to the ropes in the barn and heave them up high and fasten them to the ring on the floor and carefully slip the ring-pin in place.

Miguel and Alonso noticed how Rego never put down the leather satchel and always wore it across his chest. They looked at each other and thought the boy to be very strange that he would work so hard and still carry the satchel around with him.

Rego worked hard and grew accustomed to the thin mountain air. He finished each day covered in dust and dirt. They let him wash beside the well that stood outside the old shack each evening. His arms were sore from all the heavy sacks of potatoes. He slept on the dirt floor of the barn on top of a pile of old gunny sacks. It was not comfortable but at the end of each hard day, he fell fast asleep anyway. He was able to eat as much as he needed in the small shack with Alonso and Miguel. At the end of the week, Alonso gave him his pay.

The sun was setting on another long Saturday, and Rego dragged the last two sacks of potatoes from the fields and prepared them to be hung in the barn. He fastened one sack and heaved it high on the pulleys and then fastened it to the ring on the floor and slipped the ring-pin in place. He then heaved the second bag up high and fastened it to the other ring but he misplaced the ring-pin. He gasped as he searched around the barn. He finally saw the metal pin behind him a few feet away but out of his reach. He carefully placed the rope on the floor and put his weight on it to keep the sack suspended high above. He stretched as far as he could to retrieve the pin and grabbed it. He straightened himself with a victorious smile. "Gotcha," he said to himself triumphantly.

"I'll take that satchel from you now, kid," a voice said from behind him. Startled, Rego glanced over his shoulder to see Miguel standing just inside the barn door, holding a machete. Alonso stepped inside the door beside Miguel, also holding a machete, "And we'll take back the thirty bolivianos we gave you this morning too," Alonso said firmly.

The two brothers had caught Rego completely by surprise. He began to shake and thought quickly to say something. "No, I earned this money fair and square," Rego answered nervously. "I worked like a mule while your lazy, fat brother watched me all week."

Miguel raised his machete and started to walk towards Rego. Alonso held his arm to stop him. "You did work hard, kid," Alonso said, "But what I'm really interested in is that leather case of yours." He pointed his machete towards the satchel hanging at Rego's side.

"What do you want this for? It just has my travel papers in it and such. Nothing else," Rego said innocently.

"Oh yeah, travel papers, huh?" Alonso said sarcastically. "You're a terrible liar, kid. You never let that case out of your sight. I've watched you. It's got something valuable in it alright, and now it's mine." Alonso and Miguel began to advance on Rego with their weapons.

"Wait!" Rego yelled. "Don't come any closer! I'm warning you or you'll be sorry." Rego was nervous as hell and his voice trembled.

"Oh yeah, sorry how?" Miguel insisted.

Rego's mind raced for something to say. "I'm...I'm a master of martial arts!" Rego said quickly. "And I won't be responsible for what happens to you if you don't step back!"

Miguel and Alonso laughed heartily at Rego. "That's enough bullshit out of you, kid. Hand it over."

"You forgot one thing..." Rego said. He quickly let his foot off the rope and the large sack of potatoes came crashing down on top of Miguel, startling Alonso. "Duck, asshole!"

Potatoes spilled out all over the dirt floor. Miguel lay unconscious amidst of pile of potatoes. Rego alertly picked up several potatoes and flung them at Alonso and struck him precisely in the head, knocking him to floor. "The same goes for you too, dirt bag!" Rego yelled. He scooped up Miguel's camouflage hat that lay on the floor and then ran out of the barn. He quickly jumped on the motorized scooter and sped off down the dirt road towards the city. Alonso stumbled out of the barn, holding his head, but it was too late. Rego was long gone. Alonso stood on the dirt road, cursing and swearing towards the empty road.

Rego rode as far as he could with the scooter into the city. He decided to find a fuel station and fill the tank on the scooter and the spare fuel can strapped to the back of the scooter.

He bought some food with his remaining money and stuffed it into his coat pockets. He rode as far as he could out of the city towards the Peruvian border. He found a hidden place off the old road amongst the trees and pulled the scooter over. He put on his jacket and used the satchel as a pillow and tried to get some sleep the rest of the night as he waited for the sun to rise the next morning.

The next morning, he ate some bread he had bought the night before, then pulled the scooter out of the trees and started it up. He had been riding for another hour when he spotted a small hut near the bottom of the hill. It was a guard stand at the border crossing. Next to it was a red and white lift gate.

Rego took out the camouflage hat he had taken from Miguel and placed it on his head. He then rode slowly towards the border crossing. A single Peruvian soldier stepped out of the hut, holding a rifle and wearing military fatigues and sunglasses. The soldier casually held up his hand for Rego to stop.

"State your business," the soldier said in a bored voice as Rego stepped off the scooter.

Rego snapped to attention and saluted the soldier clumsily. "Viva Velasco!" he shouted.

The soldier lifted the gate and motioned for him to go on through.

Chapter 7

Rego rode past a large lake that had an old wooden sign painted in red letters. The sign read, *Lago Titicaca*. It took him nearly a half hour to ride around the entire lake. The sun shone brightly around the lake and he could see the reflection of the clouds on the water with the mountains in the background. Rego stopped for a moment to take in the magnificent sight.

As he rode on, the snow-covered mountain peaks were all around him as he traveled on the valley roads and up and down steep mountain slopes. The air grew cold in the mountain shadows and he was always glad to emerge from the giant shadows and into the sunlight once again where it was warm. The peaks of the Andes were so numerous, he could not count them all. Rego was just amazed at such a beautiful sight.

As he rode down yet another steep incline, he felt the engine begin to sputter. He pulled over and put the last of the fuel into the tank and rode as far as he could before the engine finally ran out. He threw the scooter off to the side of the road and started to hitch-hike the rest of the way. He passed a sign that read, 'Cusco 50km'. *That's a long way to walk,* he thought. *I sure hope somebody comes along.*

The mountain air was brisk, and the wind blew hard at times as he wandered down the mountain road. It was nearing dark when some headlights appeared over the hill behind him. Rego stuck out his thumb as a vehicle approached him. A small, beat up van pulled alongside and stopped.

A woman with long, blonde hair rolled down the window on the passenger side. "Where ya headed?" she asked in English. Rego did not understand, so he stood there silently. The man in the driver seat stared at him patiently. They were both in their twenties, not much older than Rego. "Are you headed to Cusco?" she asked again.

"Cusco, sí," Rego said finally.

"Well, jump on in!" she answered happily pulling the handle on the back door. He climbed into the van and shut the door behind him.

"Name's Alex," the driver spoke up. "This is my girlfriend Andrea, I just call her Andy. We're from California!"

Crazy Americanos. Great! Rego thought. *What the hell are they doing down here?*

Andy turned way around in her seat. She had a tattoo of a peace symbol on her bare arm. Alex had a bandana tied around the top of his head. "I don't think he speaks English, Alex baby. Do you speak English?" she asked him. Rego shook his head.

"He doesn't speak English," she said turning back around in her seat.

"Well see if he's hungry. Looks like he's been walking around out here for days," Alex said, throwing some potato chips in his mouth.

Andy turned around in her seat again, holding up a bag of potato chips, "Tango ahmbray, amigo?" She smiled at him thinking her Spanish was perfectly understandable. Rego nodded and took some chips from the bag. "Look, he's eating them!" she said excitedly.

"Calm down, he's not a zoo animal," Alex scolded her. "Give him the bag and let him be."

Rego sat back and munched hungrily on the bag of chips. He was glad to relax for a while. He tried hard to ignore the curious American woman in the front seat. He closed his eyes and let the rattling of the van help him drift off to sleep.

Andy spun around in her seat again. "Hey, what's your name?" Rego jumped in his seat, startled awake by the curious Andy. He looked at her like a madwoman. He closed his eyes and didn't answer since he didn't know what she said anyway. Andy put a finger to her chin. "Let me see if I can remember how to say that in Spanish," she thought out loud.

"Leave him alone," Alex said with a yawn and slapped her finger down. She ignored him, though.

"Como se llama?" she said with assuredness.

Rego slowly opened his eyes again, thinking she would never let him rest in peace. He sat up and took a deep breath and sighed heavily, then said sleepily, "Rego."

"Hey!" Andy shrieked in delight, startling both Alex and Rego awake again. "I said it right! His name is Ringo! Alright, groovy man. He's my favorite Beatle. I love his hair."

Alex rolled his eyes at her. "He didn't say *Ringo*. He said *Reee-go*. Just turn around and leave him alone, will ya? We're almost there."

Rego just shook his head in confusion. *I wonder if all Americans are like this?* he thought to himself. *What a bunch of strange people.*

As they entered Cusco, Alex drove slowly down the narrow streets, looking for a market that was still open. He finally found one that sold fruits and fresh vegetables and an assortment of dried peppers and jerky. They bought a few bags of fruits and vegetables and even a few sticks of fresh jerky. Andy saw they had some dusty cans of Coca Cola on the shelf, so she bought a six-pack of them as well.

They came back to the van where Rego sat with his eyes closed. Alex opened the door and put the bags inside. "Hey man, we're here in Cusco now. You can hang with us if you want, but we're on our way to go camp out tonight."

Rego sat up in the seat. He had no idea what Alex was saying. He looked around the street that was dimly lit and saw the market. "Do you know how I can get to Lima?" he asked in Spanish.

Alex only understood the name Lima. "Lima? No this is Cusco, man."

Andy came hopping behind Alex, full of energy. "Hey, maybe he's on his way to Lima, maybe he's not stopping in Cusco. Aren't we going to Lima later on? That's where we head out of this place, right?"

Alex nodded and thought for a moment and then spoke up. "Listen man, you seem pretty cool to me. We're going to Lima but not for a couple of days. If you want, you can hang with us until then."

Rego tried to understand. "Lima, que?" he said curiously.

Alex turned towards Andy, "How do you say two days?"

"Dos dias, silly!" she said with a smile.

Rego sat up when he heard that. "Lima? En dos dias?" Rego smiled and nodded yes to them.

"Far out, man. Well, let's get this show on the road!" Alex said with enthusiasm. They piled into the van and headed out of Cusco. They drove for another hour and then stopped in a heavily wooded area. He found a good place to pull over on the side of the road that had a lot of tree cover. Alex and Andy grabbed one of the bags of food and then pulled an old tent from the back of the van. Andy went dancing into the trees, still full of energy. Alex grabbed a small flashlight and started to follow her, then turned around to look at Rego still sitting inside the van.

"Looks like you've got the van to yourself, my man. Stretch out in here if you want, we're going to go set up our tent out there somewhere. See you in the morning!" Andy said with a wink.

Rego watched as Alex disappeared into the trees with the flashlight. He could still hear Andy singing to herself out in the night with delight. He breathed a heavy sigh of relief. *Finally, some peace and quiet to myself,* he thought to himself. Then he shut the door and flopped down on the long bench and was fast asleep in minutes.

The next morning it was still dark when Rego heard the back door of the van open. He slowly lifted his head over the seat to see Andy putting the rolled-up tent back inside.

"Hey, sleepy head!" she said to him cheerfully. Rego rolled his eyes and fell back on the bench.

A morning person, he thought to himself. *Of course, she is.*

Alex and Andy both jumped in the front seats and the van roared to life. They both looked at each other with excitement in their eyes.

"Are you ready, love?" Alex asked her with a growing eagerness.

"I'm ready, baby. Lost City, here we come!" she yelled with a howl.

Rego was fully awake at that point, for he had very little choice in the matter. He was curious at what all the excitement was about, though. He sat up in the seat and watched as they drove down the road. The van slowed down to a small narrow road that led up a steep hill. Alex turned up the hill and carefully made his way up the incline. He drove for a little while longer and then pulled over. Alex and Andy both jumped out in joyous anticipation. They grabbed a few belongings and food and then motioned to Rego to get out as well.

"Come on, Rego. You have to go with us! Let's get up there before the sun comes up," Andy said with glee. She reached her hand out and encouraged Rego to get out of the van. He got out of the van with a growing curiosity to where they were going.

This was the moment Andy and Alex had been waiting for. It was the single point to their entire journey from San Diego. It was the highlight of their trip. They climbed up a narrow path that winded its way up the mountain. The view behind them as the sun came up was spectacular. As they neared the top of the path, Andy started jumping up and down with joy. Rego came up behind them, panting. He looked to see what they were so gleefully pointing toward. Erected before them, was a large wooden sign that read in Spanish, *Machu Picchu – Lost City of the Incas.*

The three climbers stepped to the edge of the city and looked down upon the ruins. The whole area was covered in a thick morning fog. They stood in awe as the fog slowly lifted in certain places, one section at a time, slowly revealing the ancient ruins of the lost city. Rego stood in amazement at the sight. He had heard the name of this place in some of his old history classes in school but never gave much thought to it. Never in his dreams did he think he would ever see it.

The sun began to rise over the ancient walls. They walked all around looking at the different rock structures and walls. They marveled at the cunning architecture and ancient engineering. Each stone in the ancient walls was carefully placed, one by one, with precise craftsmanship. Each wall had not a trace of mud or mortar. The city was an architectural wonder.

Soon, other people showed up to walk around the ruins as the sun lifted high. The three of them found a place to sit on the wall to eat some lunch. They opened the bag of food and pulled out oranges and apples from the market and passed them around. Rego sat with an apple in his hand, looking down over the marvelous site. Alex had carried a small ukulele with him all the way up the mountain side. He pulled it out and started to play a tune while Andy started to hum along with him, waving her head back and forth with her hair flowing in the air. He played a tune they had written together and soon Andy started to sing the words as he played.

So, I'm singing, flying
I'm just like a bird that flies
Into your waiting arms
With flowers, daisies
In your precious garden
With the butterflies

63

Way up in the skies
I'm soaring with your love
Upon my lips
You kiss me
Sweetly
High above the ocean

Rego listened as she sang and thought her voice sounded very nice. He stared out into the open view while he listened to the tune they played. He thought about Rosa in Brasilia, wishing that she were here to see this wonderful sight with him. He didn't find Andy so annoying any longer. He began to appreciate their excitement and shared it with them. *It was a great idea to come up here,* he thought to himself.

They spent the whole day wandering around Machu Picchu. Late in the afternoon, the local caretakers began asking the visitors to start heading back down the mountain. A light rain started to fall as the three explorers made their way back down the mountain.

It was nearly dark when they reached the van. They were all tired from the climbing and exploring the ruins all day. Alex pulled the van out and drove down the narrow road and made it back to the main road to Lima. He drove a few blocks and pulled over to the side.

"Hey man, you want to drive us the rest of the way to Lima?" he asked, turning all the way around in his seat to face Rego. Rego looked at him blankly. "You, drive to Lima?" he asked him again, motioning with his hands as if he was holding a steering wheel. Rego finally understood as Alex hopped out of the driver side door. Rego climbed into the driver seat. As he looked over the gears and pedals, Andy slipped out of her seat and crawled to the back seat and waited for Alex to get in. Rego watched as she slithered to the back with a sheepish grin on her face.

Rego pulled the van out onto the dark road and started towards Lima. He could hear Alex and Andy behind him, playfully kissing and making out passionately in the back seat. Rego immediately felt embarrassed. He shook his head as he drove and mumbled quietly to himself, "Crazy Americanos."

Rego drove most of the night until he could see the sky begin to glow up ahead. He could tell the lights of the big city were up ahead. His eyes were weary, and he rubbed them to try and stay alert. The activity in the back seat had quieted down and Andy slept with her head rested on Alex's shoulder. Alex was asleep with his head against the window.

They pulled into the city just before sunrise. Rego found a busy square to pull into and he stopped alongside a park in the middle. He turned around to see Alex and Andy just opening their eyes.

"Good morning, friends. Welcome to Lima," he said with a smile. Andy smiled back at him.

"Well, we made it, didn't we?" she said smiling and stretching her arms. "I suppose you are going to leave now?" Rego gathered up his jacket and the leather satchel and opened the driver door. "I'll take that as a yes," she said smartly.

Alex and Andy crawled out of the van and Rego met them on the other side. He smiled at them and reached out his hand to Alex to shake his hand. "Gracias, mis amigos, gracias," he said to them. He shook his hand, and then he smiled once more at Andy. Andy then gave Rego a hug, which he didn't expect.

"You take care, amigo! And don't forget to write," she said with a beaming smile.

Chapter 8

Rego was very tired as he walked through the streets of Lima. The business of everyday life went on all around him. He thought he would see signs of military occupation and strife in Lima, but he did not. It was nothing like what Alonso had described back in Bolivia. People hurried by on bicycles, motor scooters and small cars. Others walked past, never taking any notice to him. The buildings were all light and beige with TV antennas scattered across the sky line on the roofs of the villas.

He wasn't too hungry, for his friends had given him a few more pieces of fruit before he had left them. What he really wanted was to find a place where he could just sit for a while and take a nap. He walked down a neighborhood street where he could hear kids laughing and playing. He came upon the source of the laughter and a smile appeared on his face. In a large open dirt lot, several kids were playing a game of football. He walked over to a small wooden set of bleachers and he sat down on them to watch them play. He thought of running out onto the field to join them in the game, but he was too tired. So, he just sat and watched as they played. After a while, he closed his eyes and faded off into a light sleep under the warm sun.

Rego slept for what seemed like hours beside the football field. Out of nowhere, he heard the voice of a child, "Hey mister, are you dead?" Rego shaded his eyes from the sun and looked all around. Finally, he saw a little boy down on the ground, sitting on a football. He was no more than eight.

"No, I'm not dead. Not yet at least," Rego said waking up.

The little boy looked at him with a curious grin, "You looked like you were dead."

Rego looked at the playing field where the kids were still playing their game. He wondered why the little boy wasn't playing too.

"What's your name?" the boy asked.

"My name is Rego. What's yours?"

"Pelé! I am the greatest football player in the world!" he pronounced loudly. He stood up and started kicking the ball around. Rego chuckled to himself at the little boy's enthusiasm.

"Pelé is my favorite player too," Rego said with a smile. "I am from the same country as he is, did you know that?" The little boy shook his head. Rego watched him kick the ball around some more. "Why aren't you out there playing the game with the other kids? You look like a good player to me?"

The little boy stared at the ground and pouted. "They say I am too little and can't play with them." He kicked some dirt on the ball.

Rego found his strength coming back to him and he felt rested enough to get a little exercise. He glanced at Pelé with a slight grin and asked him, "Can I kick the ball with you?"

Pelé readily agreed and Rego jumped from the bleachers and put his jacket on the ground. He swung the satchel across his chest. They began kicking the ball back and forth to one another on the side of the playing field.

"You're pretty good, little Pelé," Rego complemented him as he kicked the ball with the side of his foot. Rego was very happy to be kicking a ball around and so was Pelé. No one had ever asked him to kick the ball around before. Rego stopped the ball with his foot and rested it on top of the ball. "Hey, do you want me to show you how to dribble the ball and set up for a shot? You learn this, and the goal keeper will never see what is coming." Pelé smiled and nodded eagerly.

Rego showed Pelé the technique of dribbling the ball, kicking it behind his legs to change directions, faking one way and going another, and then taking aim at the net. Pelé learned quickly and loved being shown the old tricks of the trade. They ran up and down the side of the field, taking turns dribbling the ball down the field.

After a while, Rego noticed that the game on the dirt lot had come to an end and the other kids had left. "Hey, Pelé, do you want to go try your new moves on a real goal?"

Pelé grabbed the ball and went running onto the field. He started kicking the ball the way he was shown and kicked it into the net. He jumped up and down and celebrated his goal. Rego trotted onto the field after him.

"Ok, I will be the goal keeper. You dribble it down and kick it past me just like I showed you," Rego yelled out to him.

Pelé ran back about thirty yards and started dribbling the ball down the field towards the goal. He got closer and closer and then stopped and faked one way and then kicked the ball perfectly past Rego's outstretched arms and into the net. They both jumped up and down and celebrated the goal. The sun began to set but Rego and Pelé continued to practice and have fun.

"I think it's getting a little dark, Pelé," Rego said, catching his breath. Pelé had worn him out. "You had better go on home or your parents will worry."

Pelé pointed towards the side of the bleachers and said, "That's my papa right there."

Rego looked to see an older man walking towards the field, carrying a lunchbox. He had just arrived at the nearby bus stop, coming home from work. Pelé started dribbling the ball over to where he stood and Rego walked behind him.

"Papa!" Pelé said out loud and hugged his father's legs. "This is my new coach, Rego!" he said enthusiastically.

The man looked at Rego tiredly. "I am Anton. You've been looking after Pelé, have you?"

"Hello, sir. I suppose I have," Rego answered. "I was just watching the game and saw that he wanted to play, so we practiced some after the game was over."

"They never ask him to play. He is so little for his age, you know?" Anton said in a tired voice. "Thank you for watching him. Do you live nearby?"

"No sir, I had better be going," Rego said picking up his jacket.

"Papa, can he come with us? I want to show you what he taught me," Pelé pleaded with his father.

"No, I better go, Pelé. It's getting late." Rego said to him. The pouting face reappeared again. "You keep practicing those moves though, ok?" Pelé wouldn't look up and stared at the ground. "A pleasure to meet you sir, good night." Rego turned to walk towards the bus stop. He walked about half way and then turned around.

"Hey Pelé, wait!" he called out to the boy and his father walking towards home. He ran to them and reached into his jacket. "I have something for you that I want you to keep." He looked at Anton, "Do you mind, sir?" Anton shrugged his shoulders. Rego pulled out his trading card with a picture of Pelé and handed it to little Pelé. "Here, I want you to have it."

Little Pelé's eyes grew wide and his mouth flew open. "Wow! It's a picture of my favorite player!" He showed it to his father proudly. Rego was pleased with his reaction.

Anton smiled at his son and looked at Rego, "Are you sure you won't come have dinner with us?"

"I would be honored, sir, but I must go. But, if you don't mind, could you tell me the best way to get to the port and loading docks?" Rego asked him.

"Yes, wait for the number eight bus there. It will be the last bus to go down to the shipping docks," he directed Rego. "But if you cannot stay, then please, my pass is still good for the rest of the day. Take it and use it when the bus arrives." He took out his old bus pass and handed it to Rego.

"Many thanks, sir," he said to Anton. "You are very kind." He looked at Pelé still admiring the trading card. "Cheer on Pelé for me when the matches begin next week, ok?"

I will!" Pelé shouted as they turned to walk home. "Go Pelé! Go Brazil!"

Anton smiled curiously at his son. "Don't you want Peru to win as well?" he asked as he laughed at his son.

Rego laughed as they walked away. He headed towards the bus stop and sat down to wait for the bus to arrive.

Rego rode on the bus with his head rested against the window. The bus was mostly empty as it rattled down the streets of Lima, slowly rolling towards the bay.

His eyes were weary, and he grew tired from the long journey. He stared down at the leather satchel sitting next to him on the seat. It had started to look worn and dirty from the rain and wind and the dirt from working in the fields. He wondered if his long journey was going to be worth all his trials and tribulations, all for the sake of something that he couldn't look at.

He took a deep breath and sighed softly to himself. All he wanted now was to rest. The sun was completely set now, and the street lights were bright as he neared the port of Lima. The bus roared past an old rusty sign that read, 'Puerto Callao'. Over in the dark distance, he could see massive structures lined along the sea wall, one after another. Rego sat up in his seat to look at them more carefully. As the bus drew nearer, he could start to make out the shape of giant ships in the darkness. He breathed another heavy sigh of relief as the bus pulled into the final stop at the port. He also felt a feeling of nervousness. He had never been on a ship before, not even a small boat. That was the least of his worries at the moment. His first task would be to find a ship that was going north and an employer that would allow him to come aboard and work.

Rego dragged himself off the bus and tried to get his bearings. Even though it was night, the port was busy with work. Men worked all through the night to get the ships loaded or unloaded in preparation to send them back out to sea.

Rego walked up and down the boardwalk, observing all the activity going on. He watched as men loaded crates with cranes, scrubbed the decks of the ships, scrubbed the exterior of the ships and even re-painted the sides. He had never seen such massive hunks of iron, and so close-up. He noticed military men patrolling the area as well. It was the first sign of the new government Alonso had spoken of that had taken over the country less than two years earlier. They wore navy blue berets and dark green uniforms, and all of them wore dark glasses, even at night. Rego looked at the lights all around the docks and shrugged his shoulders. *They don't seem that bright,* he thought to himself.

He stopped for a moment when he saw a bench out of the way. So, he decided to rest for a while and just watch all the activity around him. Across the boardwalk from him were some smaller boats with Peruvian flags on them. Rego just assumed they were for the military men or harbor patrol boats. He observed two workers enter a small wooden building with no markings on it. He wondered if it was an office of some type. Maybe it was the place where he could ask about employment. About ten minutes had passed, when the two men emerged from the building, dressed in the military uniforms and dark glasses and carrying small rifles.

Rego sat up on the bench and watched them closely. They walked down a pier with two other civilian workers and stepped onto one of the small boats with the Peruvian flags. Another flag was raised under the Peruvian flag. It was marked with plain red and white colors. Soon, the boat began to pull away from the pier and head out into the bay. A large sign on top of the vessel read in English and Spanish letters, *Harbor Pilot.* Rego was intrigued, he wondered what the harbor pilot's job was. He got up from the bench and watched the small boat slowly ride out towards the mouth of the bay. He walked along the boardwalk trying to keep it within sight, though the darkness made it more difficult to follow. The small boat approached a massive ship that had just entered the bay. It pulled alongside the ship and suddenly, a long rope ladder fell from the deck of the ship down to the harbor pilot vessel. Soon, one of the soldiers began to climb the rope ladder, followed by one of the civilian workers. They both reached the top of the deck and disappeared onto the ship. The rope ladder was quickly hauled up and the harbor pilot vessel slowly pulled away from the ship. He watched as the giant floating piece of iron slowly approached the dock area. After a long while, the large ship came to rest in a space along the docks.

Rego was impressed and nodded in understanding. "I get it now," he thought out loud, "he's the valet!"

After watching the large ship come in, he walked some more around the port and began noticing the markings on the stern of each ship. Some of them had the name of the company that owned the ship, others did not, but all of them had what Rego was looking for, the country of origin of each ship. He saw names of all kinds, Columbia, Mexico, Argentina, United States, Chile, and even Brazil. Then he saw names of places even farther away, like the Philippines, Japan, and New Zealand. Then a ship with another familiar name caught his eye. A smaller, yet still very large ship painted black and red across the stern. In huge, white, capital letters the name, *PANAMA*, was painted on the back.

Rego scratched his chin and thought to himself, *This is the one. It has to be.*

He finally came across a building with the word *Oficina* written on the door. He walked into the small office and saw a clerk sitting behind a desk. The clerk paid no attention to him and kept working.

"Excuse me, sir," Rego said politely, "is this where I apply for a job on one of the ships? I was told the one going to Panama was looking for help."

"Is that so?" the night clerk said, still looking down at his work. "Can't help you here, kid. You have to go talk to the ship's first mate for that kind of work."

"Do you know where I can find him?" asked Rego.

The night clerk finally looked at Rego with an annoyed expression. "Just look for the man holding a clipboard, kid. Now can you beat it? I'm busy."

Rego slowly left the office with a discouraged look on his face. He walked out on the boardwalk and looked towards the ship from Panama. A large crane was lifting wooden crates to the deck of the ship. He looked around, hoping to see a man that looked to be in charge. A small group of workers talked near the ship, but none held a clipboard. He neared the gang plank that led to the deck of the ship and then he saw a man in a dark blue dress shirt strolling very quickly down the gang plank to the boardwalk. He had a pencil behind his ear and carried a wooden clipboard at his side. Rego immediately started to walk faster and tried to get to the bottom of the walkway as soon as the man did.

"Hello, sir?" Rego said nervously. "They told me at the office you were the man to talk to about a job on this ship."

The man didn't stop walking. He headed towards the bow of the ship. He gave a quick look to Rego who was trying to keep up. "Got no work here, kid. Sorry."

"I'm a hard worker, sir. I can do whatever you need. I'm a born seaman," Rego said with pride.

The first mate stopped, he could tell he wouldn't be able to get rid of Rego very easily. "Listen kid, I told you I don't need anybody." He looked Rego up and down. He noticed all he had with him was a jacket and a satchel. "Listen, you look like an honest kid. I'm a busy man, so I'll give you one minute. What can you do for me? You ever worked on a ship before?"

Rego perked up. "Oh yes, sir! I can scrub the decks, clean the sides, whatever you need." He quickly looked around trying to think of something else. He caught a glimpse of the moor lines coming from the ship to the dock. "And, I can help the crew secure the lines, sir. I'll work long hours, no problem!" He snapped to attention and saluted the first mate.

The man put his hands on his hips and looked at him with a crooked stare. "I don't need any clowns around here, kid."

Somewhat embarrassed, Rego put his arm down. "Yes, I'm sorry, sir. Please, I'm a hard worker, really. I just need a job."

He looked Rego over one last time. "Are you gonna give me any trouble, kid?"

"No, sir!"

"Be here at six A.M. sharp," the first mate barked. "We're on a tight schedule and we have to unload these crates in Panama City in two days. Ship leaves at seven!" He strode off towards the end of the ship, pulling the pencil from his ear and scribbled something on his clipboard.

Rego smiled in relief. "Yes, sir," he called out. "I will be here!"

The next morning, Rego was out on the boardwalk well before six A.M. He had slept for a few hours at the bus stop until the buses began to arrive and he had to leave. He peeled an orange over a trashcan, wiping the sleep from his eyes. He couldn't believe he was actually going to board a ship and head out to sea.

He ate the orange as he walked down the boardwalk towards the Panamanian ship. He saw the man he had spoken to the night before, barking orders at workers all around him. He was going over last-minute details before they set sail. Rego walked up beside him and waited for him to finish yelling out orders. He had already noticed Rego coming down the boardwalk.

"Get these mats squared away! I want these moor lines un-cabled in fifteen minutes!" He shot a quick glance at Rego and pulled a slip of paper from his clipboard. "Take this to the office, kid, and give them your name with the ship number. It's on the top there," pointing quickly at the sheet of the paper. "Get checked in and be back here, pronto!" He turned back to the workers, "Come on men, I don't have all day. Get this crap hauled off the deck!"

Rego turned towards the office and trotted a few hundred yards and froze in his tracks. Opening the door to the office was Coutier. He had just arrived in Lima by plane the night before. He had gotten word from Gomes and LaBonne about the bus incident and now knew Rego was heading to the west coast somewhere.

Rego's heart began to pound in his chest. He watched as Coutier went inside the office. *How did that bastard find me here?* he thought to himself. His mind raced for answers on what to do. His ticket out of here was that ship and he had to be on it by the time it left. He walked quickly past the office and down the boardwalk and then slipped behind a metal warehouse. He leaned up against a wall and then saw a large empty oil drum. So, he crouched down behind it and peered around the edge to keep a lookout. He sat thinking as fast as he could on what he should do. He *had* to get on that ship. He thought about the first mate who had given him the job. *He must be wondering where I am by now,* he thought to himself. *If he talks to the agent, he will turn me in for sure.*

Coutier approached the clerk and held up a composite drawing of Rego. The clerk was a different man from the night before. "Have you seen this man?" he snapped.

"No sir, never," the clerk said calmly. "But, maybe the night clerk saw him, who knows?" Coutier turned and angrily walked out of the office.

Rego waited impatiently as the minutes passed. He gathered his courage and stood up behind the oil drum. He slowly walked out from behind the warehouse and looked around cautiously. He saw his ship and the moor lines were now raised and release water poured from the side of the ship. It was on the verge of pulling away from the dock. Then he spotted Coutier walking down the boardwalk with a sheet of paper in his hands, holding it up to every person he passed. He turned to walk the opposite way, but he spotted Gomes and LaBonne walking the other way down the boardwalk doing the same thing as Coutier. LaBonne walked with a neck brace and Rego grinned, remembering the crash they encountered with the tree.

Shit. They are all over the place, he thought to himself. He pressed against the side of the wall again, breathing heavily. He looked at the satchel hanging across his chest. "Damn," he muttered under his breath, "I've come this far."

He stepped onto the boardwalk and slowly walked away from the ship, trying not to be seen. He began to panic when he noticed his ship started to pull away from the dock.

Then, looking the other way up the boardwalk, he got an idea. He quickly walked back up the boardwalk behind Gomes and LaBonne, staying out of sight. He sat down on the bench where he sat the night before and stared at the military building. Soon, two soldiers emerged from the building wearing sunglasses and carrying rifles. When their backs turned, Rego raced to the building and slipped inside. The room was empty, but luckily, he found what he was looking for. Several uniforms hung on the wall over by a stack of metal lockers. He quickly threw one on over his clothes and satchel. He grabbed a navy-blue beret, placed it on his head and quickly snatched a rifle from a gun case and ran out of the building.

The two soldiers were already walking down the pier towards the harbor pilot vessel. Rego found a pair of sunglasses in the front pocket of the uniform and he put them on. He ran down the pier and caught up with the two soldiers and strode along behind them as if he knew what he was doing.

He climbed aboard the boat behind them and one of them turned around. "Private Ouliveyra reporting for duty, sir." he said firmly, saluting the soldier. "I'm here to learn the ropes!"

The soldier looked at him curiously and then at the other soldier and snapped, "You didn't tell me we had a rookie this morning. Damn that corporal. He never keeps us informed."

The other soldier looked at him blankly. "Cast off!" was the shout from the captain. The soldier looked at Rego and ordered, "Man your post, soldier!" Rego stepped to the front of the boat and held his rifle firmly to his chest.

The boat pulled into the bay and headed towards the black and red ship heading for Panama. The captain steered the boat alongside the massive ship. Rego was astonished at the sheer size of the vessel. His nerves grew more tense as they approached. Soon, a rope ladder came falling to the deck. The harbor pilot stepped out of the cabin and made his way over to the ladder. Rego alertly stepped up to the ladder, but the soldier standing next to him pulled him back.

Rego thought quickly, "I will go, sir. It's the only way for me to learn." The other soldier looked at him sternly. There was little time to argue.

"Get up there, soldier!" he barked. Rego immediately flung his rifle over his shoulder and began climbing the ladder to the ship. The harbor pilot followed close behind. Rego finally reached the top of the deck and was out of breath. He stood at attention as best as he could as the harbor pilot climbed up behind him. One of the other soldiers followed him up the ladder and stepped aboard the ship. He approached Rego and said, "Let's go."

They walked behind the pilot as he made his way to the bridge. They stopped outside the main door. "You wait here," he commanded. "I will escort the pilot to the bridge."

Rego stood guard outside the door. He couldn't believe he had made it on board. It wasn't until now that he realized how large the ship was. He didn't even notice while he climbed the long rope ladder, he was just trying to climb as fast as he could. He was overwhelmed at how high the ship towered over the water. He could barely contain his amazement. *Boy, this ship is humongous,* he thought to himself. He took deep breath to calm his nerves and began to look around the deck. He needed to get rid of the uniform and gun and try to blend in with the crew somehow. He looked up and down the deck of the ship and saw workers all around still securing the lines below the decks. The first mate came walking down the walkway right towards him. Rego's eyes grew wide but he kept his composure. He walked right past Rego and never looked up from his clipboard. Rego slowly side-stepped his way down the walkway, looking for a place to duck into. Suddenly a worker came up behind him. Rego saluted the old man and said, "I'm heading back to the ladder, I am very sick." The old man shrugged his shoulders as though he didn't care.

Rego strode off towards the back of the ship where the harbor pilot vessel waited. Before he reached the ladder, he slipped into a room he had noticed when they came aboard. It was a mechanical room full of barrels and other cleaning tools. He quickly took off the uniform and stuffed it and the rifle into one of the barrels and closed the lid. He opened the door slowly and stepped onto the deck and found the nearest staircase to a lower level.

The ship was free of the harbor and was now headed northward. The pilot and the soldier exited the bridge and made their way back to the ladder. The soldier looked all around for Rego but didn't see him. He continued to follow the pilot to the ladder. He saw the old man standing at the ladder. "Did you see the other soldier on the deck?"

"Oh yeah, he went back down because he got seasick," the man laughed. The soldier looked over the side but couldn't see well to the boat below as tit was too far down. He swore under his breath and then stepped over the side onto the ladder. The two men reached the boat below and it quickly pulled away.

The old man on deck pulled the ladder up. He looked down at the boat pulling away and saw the two soldiers yelling at each other and pointing upward. The man laughed as he finished pulling the rope ladder back up. "I guess that rookie won't be back," he laughed to himself.

Rego calmed down and began to walk around the ship to learn his way around. He walked to the maintenance deck where a lot of men were working, stowing away the moor lines. Just then, the first mate appeared on the deck. Rego immediately grabbed a push broom that was leaning against the wall.

The first mate spotted Rego as he walked past. "Where the hell you been, mister?" he shouted angrily.

"Just sweeping up and helping the men secure the lines, sir," he answered with confidence.

"Bullshit, kid. You check in with me before you board this vessel, you hear me? Don't you ever leave me waiting around again. Now get back to work!" He stormed off in a huff.

Rego smiled and breathed a huge sigh of relief as he watched the first mate disappear around a corner. He had made it.

Coutier, LaBonne, and Gomes returned to the port office that evening. There was one more person they wanted to question. The night clerk that Rego had spoken to the night before sat behind the old wooden counter.

Coutier approached him with a smile and held the drawing in front of the clerk's face, "Have you seen this man?"

The clerk stared the picture with immediate recognition, saying, "Yes, yes, I've seen this man. He was in here just last night asking for a job on a ship."

Coutier crumpled the paper in his hands and the clerk looked at him as if he were crazy. "*What* ship?" Coutier snarled.

Chapter 9

The sea was calm, and the sun was bright as the ship headed northward to Panama. Rego slowly adjusted to the movement of the ship as he worked and soon learned to not think about it. To keep from getting motion sickness, he would take a break from his work and stare out to the shore and watch it go by as they slowly sailed onward.

Rego went from one deck to the next, mopping the floors of the walkways that ran along the sides of the ship. The sea wasn't rough, but the ship still rocked from side to side at times. After a while, Rego stopped mopping and had to rest. He leaned over the side and thought he might be sick, but he took in deep breaths and soon he started feeling better.

"This is your first time on a ship, isn't it?" a voice said behind him. Rego slowly turned his head to the side to see who it was. A young sailor stood behind him wearing a black cap and a broad grin on his face.

"What's makes you say that?" Rego asked, straightening himself out.

"You haven't gotten your sea legs yet," the young man answered. "You're stumbling all over the place. But that's ok, you'll get used to it." He stuck his hand out to shake Rego's hand, "I'm Doc, the ship's steward. Who are you?"

"I'm Rego, the ship's captain," he quipped, shaking his hand.

"Ha! You're a quick witted one, aren't you?" Doc said laughing.

"Look Captain, don't stare at the water like that, it'll just make it worse. Just act normal and everything will be fine." They both sat down on a long bench that ran along the far wall. "So, where you headed?"

Rego looked at him with suspicion. "I'm just here to work. I'm not going anywhere in particular."

"Sure, you are," Doc replied. "Everybody on here is going somewhere. The ship owners don't care, just as long as they have a crew on each voyage to get this cargo where they need to."

"Well, I guess you are right," Rego said. "Right now, I am just going to Panama. So, what does a steward do?" Rego wanted to change the subject.

"I take care of the provisions on the ship. Keep everybody fed and make sure everybody has a bunk to sleep on. I have a lot of time in between though," Doc said staring out to sea. "I live in Panama, you'll like it there." He stood up and looked at Rego sympathetically. "Hang in there, Captain, you'll make it. Time to get back to work." He left Rego sitting there alone.

Rego thought about what Doc had told him to deal with the motion of the ship. Rego nodded, thinking it wasn't such a bad idea. "Just act normal, huh?" he asked himself. "Don't stare at the water. Ok, we can do this, Rego, old boy." After a few more moments he nodded confidently and stood and grabbed the mop and bucket.

Rego found where the bunks were for the crew and threw himself on an empty one. He was so tired he could probably sleep standing up. A few more crew members started to come into the barracks. They talked amongst themselves and paid little attention to him. He lay on his bunk for a while with his eyes closed. He could feel the movement of the ship as he lay on his back. It slowly rocked him to sleep.

After a few hours, his eyes opened and found he was the only one in the barracks. He looked over at an old clock hanging on the wall that read half past seven. He felt hungry and he assumed all the other crew was down in the galley having dinner. What he really needed most though, was to wake up. He wandered down to the end of the barracks, where he found the bathroom. Opposite of the stalls were five small shower heads lining a ceramic wall. *A shower*, he thought. *That's what I need*. The water was cold but Rego didn't care. He let the water fall on his head as he leaned on his arm against the ceramic wall. After all the hours of mopping the decks, and all the things he had been through since he left Brasilia, Rego had started to show signs of wearing down. The cold water reinvigorated him, though, and gave him some time to gather his strength. He thought about his grandmother and Rosa and hoped that Rosa was looking after her well. He couldn't believe he had been away from home for so long now.

After he dressed, he walked down to the galley where a few men were eating. He grabbed a tray and slowly slid it down the buffet line. There was very little food left, just a few pieces of dried bread and two pieces of baked fish.

"Rego, where have you been? The galley closes at eight, you know," Doc said from behind the counter. "You barely made it, my friend."

Rego did not realize he had almost missed dinner. "Oh yeah, sorry. I fell asleep and lost track of time." He put the plate down on his tray and grabbed a glass of water and then sat at the nearest table by himself. He was famished so he quickly devoured the fish and bread.

The kitchen detail had already started cleaning the buffet trays and dishes at the sink. Doc came out from behind the counter and sat across from Rego and watched him eat. He produced another piece of bread on another plate and slid it over to Rego. "Here, we had one more piece left over." Rego nodded in thanks and quickly scarfed it down.

"So, what are you going to do tomorrow?" he asked Rego.

Rego kept eating the bread and said without looking up, "I have an early date with a mop in the morning. Why?"

"Well, we are all day at sea tomorrow before we reach Panama City. If we get our work done, the captain will sometimes let us do some trap shooting from the stern. You want to come join us?" Doc asked him.

Rego had never shot a gun before, but it sounded interesting to him. A lot better than mopping the decks. "Sure, sounds like fun to me," he responded.

"We'll be in Panama City by Saturday afternoon. It will be mad with people. The matches are in Mexico this year and people will be streaming through from all over South America," Doc said leaning on his elbow.

Rego perked up when he mentioned the World Cup. "You're right, the first match is Saturday. Brazil's first match is the following Wednesday. I hope I get to see some of it."

Doc raised one eyebrow, "Ah, a Brazilian, I knew it! I had a feeling that accent wasn't Peruvian. You get around my friend. What part of Brazil are you from?"

"Brasilia," Rego said, acknowledging his interest. "We are going to win it this time, I just know it."

"Perhaps, but my money is on Peru. They have a good squad this year," Doc said with a smile. He looked Rego over and began to wonder why he was so far away from his home. "So, what's next once you get to Panama?"

"I don't know. Look for another way to keep going, I guess," Rego said with a yawn. He didn't want to divulge too much but he was so tired, it was hard not to talk about his journey.

"Keep going? Where are you off to next?" Doc kept prying. He could tell Rego did not want to say too much. Doc's eyes lifted as if a revelation came upon him. "Ah, I see what's going on. A young man who wants to see the world, right?"

Rego looked at Doc and shrugged his shoulders, "Yeah, I guess you could say that." He thought for a moment if he should tell him anymore. He thought of the map that he and Rosa had looked at in the library. He finally decided to tell some of his plans. "I had always wanted to see the Mediterranean. I plan to head that way, maybe to Greece. Then after I see what I want, I'll go back home."

"I love it," Doc said in admiration. "A true journeyman. Just throwing caution to the wind and exploring the world. I like your style, my friend." He stood and glanced toward his cleaning crew. "I need to get back to the kitchen. We'll come find you tomorrow when we start to shoot the traps."

"Ok, thanks, I'll see you then." Rego put his tray at the window and headed back to the barracks. He was still exhausted.

Rego didn't have an alarm clock, but he didn't need one. The wake-up alarm on the wall sounded above their heads at six a.m. sharp. Rego threw his pillow over his head until it stopped. All the other crew started climbing out of their bunks.

Rego groaned out loud in a desperate attempt to go back to sleep. "Ohhhhh, shit! What the hell was that?" he moaned out loud.

"Wake up call," said Ramon, a young Mexican on the bunk above his head. He worked in the machine rooms in the bowels of the ship. "They have biscuits in the galley. Then, it's off to work at six forty-five. Better hurry, before they are all gone." Ramon bounced off his bunk and dashed down the aisle, throwing on his shoes. Rego found his clothes and his shoes and stumbled his way to the galley, throwing his satchel around his shoulders.

Rego jumped into the line in the galley for the biscuits and cream gravy. He tried to pat his hair down as best he could while moving through the line. Doc stood behind the counter, handing plates of biscuits and gravy to the men. "Ah, you are learning my friend," he said, seeing Rego. "You made it on time I see." Doc handed him a plate. He stared at the satchel around Rego's shoulders as he moved down the line.

Rego stood with his mop and bucket and continued mopping D deck. The sky was clear, and the wind rushed by as the ship continued north. He liked to stare at the coastline from the starboard side as they slowly passed by. He wondered what country it was that they were passing. Ecuador, perhaps Columbia. Soon, he noticed that the coast began to look farther and farther away.

A few hours had passed, and he had finished his mopping of the decks. He closed the door to the maintenance room and turned to walk up the stairs to C deck when he saw Doc coming down with two other young men.

"Hey, we were just looking for you. The captain said we can go shoot some traps from the stern on this deck. You done with the mops?" Doc asked Rego.

"As done as I'll ever be," Rego said.

"This is Antonio and Franklin from the kitchen," he said introducing them to Rego. "They are sharpshooters."

They headed up to A deck and walked to the back of the ship where another crew member was setting up an old skeet launcher. The ocean rushed by as Rego leaned against the rail and watched as they prepared the launcher. He watched as Antonio loaded the rifle and waited for the launch. The traps were round clay discs painted yellow, just a little bit larger than a saucer.

"Ever shoot one of these before?" Doc asked leaning against the rail next to Rego.

"No," he said watching Antonio intently.

Antonio lifted the gun to his shoulder and then shouted to the launcher, "Pull!" A loud metallic sound came from the contraption and with a quick motion of the swing-arm, one yellow disk went sailing into the air thirty meters out. Within seconds, Antonio fired a single round from the rifle and the disk shattered in the air and scattered softly into the ocean. He cocked the rifle again, lifted it to his shoulder and shouted once more,

"Pull!" Again, the disk was shattered, trying to escape the ship. Antonio lowered his rifle with a confident grin, and then offered the rifle to Rego.

Rego clumsily opened the rifle and loaded two rounds as Antonio had done earlier, then finally lifted the rifle to his shoulder.

"Maybe you should take that thing off your shoulder, it will get in the way," Doc said, referring to the satchel around Rego's shoulder.

"No, it's fine. Pull!" he shouted, and the disc was launched. He took his best aim at the flying saucer and then squeezed off a single shot, not knowing if he would even come close to hitting it. The shot rang out, but the disc continued to sail out and then fade slowly down to the water. Rego frowned but he had a feeling that would be the result. He watched as the disc softly landed on the surface and slowly disappeared under the waves.

Antonio spoke up, seeing it was his first try, "It's alright, try another shot. Keep it in your scope. But, you have to lead it a little."

Rego took the advice with a frown, but he was determined. "Lead it a little," he muttered to himself." He lifted his rifle and shouted once again, "Pull!" The disk went sailing into the air and Rego followed it in his scope and then pulled the trigger. To his shock, the disc exploded in the air. Rego whirled around in delight, "I hit it!" All three men ducked because the gun was pointed straight at them when he whirled around.

Doc pushed the barrel of the gun to the side with a worried grin, "Hey, watch the barrel there, cowboy. Point that thing down when you're done. Nice shot though." Rego looked embarrassed when he realized he was pointing the empty gun at them. He handed the rifle over to Doc and let him take a few shots.

The men took turns shooting the gun and watching the clay discs shatter in the air. Rego started to pay less attention to the trap shooting and more to the open water. He soon realized he could see land a great distance on the horizon to the west. He stood up and looked at it closer. They were large islands that looked rather flat, but he could only see the shape of the land on the horizon.

"What land is that out there?" he asked to the group of men. They all looked out in the direction Rego was pointing.

"Oh," responded Doc, "Those are the Galapagos, where all the giant tortoises live. That's where all the scientists go to look at turtles, if you can imagine that. There's nothing there but wild creatures." Rego stared at the islands for a while longer and tried to imagine what the giant turtles looked like. He wondered what it would be like to just go to a deserted island and watch the animals. He loved to daydream about such things.

The sun began to set, and the waves began to lash against the side of the ship. The clouds rolled in and a light rain began to fall. Soon, they all packed up the discs and launcher and headed back to the barracks.

Rego was fast asleep in his bunk. The storm outside on the sea grew more intense and the ship rocked from side to side. Suddenly the ship tipped even further to one side and Rego went tumbling out of his bunk and crashed onto the floor.

"*Shit*, my head!" he cursed under his breath as he lifted himself to his knees on the hard iron floor. The boat kept rocking back and forth. He noticed that he was the only one on the floor. Everyone else was still fast asleep.

Ramon leaned his head over the side of his bunk with an exasperated expression on his face. He pointed to a leather strap attached to the side of his bunk. "You have to use the straps, you idiot. Now pipe down!" He rolled back over and closed his eyes.

Rego sat on the edge of his bunk, holding his head. He dug his hand down underneath the thin mattress and pulled out the tie-down straps. He shook his swollen head and muttered to himself, "*Now* they tell me."

Chapter 10

Rego stood on A Deck with his mop and bucket and looked down at the floors in dismay. The storm from the night before had washed saltwater all over the ship's deck. The clouds had cleared away somewhat and sunshine peaked from around the remaining dark clouds in the early morning. Land was in sight and was easy to see now as they quickly approached their destination. He could see the tall palm trees and tropical vegetation up and down the coastline. He knew they must be near or even inside the waters of Panama.

The first mate came walking up briskly behind Rego. "I want these decks scrubbed clean before we make the canal, mister!" he barked at him. Rego acknowledged him with a slight nod and started mopping the deck with fresh water.

Rego worked hard through the morning. He took time out to take in the incredible tropical scenery as the ship slowly made its way up the coast into the Gulf of Panama. He could see monkeys in the trees jumping from limb to limb. Some just sat on the branches and stared at the strange vessel that passed them by on the waters. Colorful birds flew from the trees and squawked loudly as they soared through the air. Some were red with long blue tail feathers, others were green with bright yellow beaks.

Rego stopped only once for a short while to go and eat a quick lunch in the galley. He wanted to get his chores done in time to watch the ship go through the channel. Engineering was always an interest of his and he always remembered reading about the Panama Canal construction in his history classes. Now, he was about to see the canal with his own eyes, and the thought was very exciting to him.

The ship slowed its pace as it neared the city. Rego put his cleaning tools away and then quickly ran to A Deck to take in the sights. He could see the white buildings now that lined the coastal streets of Panama City. As they got closer, hundreds of people could be seen on the streets of Panama City, tourists and locals alike. Many were passing through to get to Mexico for the football matches, others were locals running their daily errands. Others were curious onlookers that came down to watch the ships pass through the canal. It was indeed a crowded place, the central corridor of the Americas from west to east, and from north to south. It was the very point for ships from all around the Pacific to enter the Atlantic. Each ship had to wait in line to take their turn to enter the Atlantic waters.

Soon, it was their turn and Rego stood high on the rail overlooking the bow as the ship neared the first lock of the canal. The gigantic lock doors slowly swung open for the ship to enter the long, narrow lock. Once inside, the water slowly began to fill the lock, lifting the mighty ship inch by inch to the next level. Rego watched in amazement as the slow process brought the ship from one lock to the next until finally they came to rest in Lake Gatun. Many of the crewmembers had gathered on the deck to watch the man-made engineering feat in motion.

Doc stepped to the railing alongside Rego and watched the lock doors slowly open as they approached the Atlantic side of the canal. "Pretty amazing, isn't it?" he asked. "I never get tired of seeing this."

Rego nodded in agreement. He glanced over at Doc, "What part of Panama do you live in?"

"I live with my family on the Caribbean side, in Colón. That's where we are going to port with this ship. I only work on ships that come to and from my home. Makes it easier, right?" he said staring out, as if he were looking right at his home.

"Sounds like a good system to me," Rego admitted. "This country is beautiful. And the canal is amazing. I've never seen anything like it.'

"The pride of Panama," Doc said proudly. "This is where the whole world comes together. Where are you going to stay while you are here, before you find your next ship?"

Rego didn't really know the answer to that question. "I don't know, I hadn't thought about it until now. Do you know anything about the ships going across the Atlantic?"

Doc answered him right away. "I know many people who work on ships in the Atlantic, but ones that go to Greece, that's another story. I will see what I can find out once we land. How soon do you want to depart?"

Rego knew the answer to that one. He most certainly wanted to leave as soon as possible. He knew he was less than half way there. "I'd love to stay in this great place, but I need to keep moving on. I will look for a way to get there as soon as we land. Do you think our pay will be enough to get a room for a night or two?"

Doc shook his head, "I doubt it, not the pay from this ship." Doc thought to himself and then turned to Rego, "How about if you stay at my parent's place in Colón? We have a couch that you can sleep on."

"Are you sure that won't be too much trouble for them? I can pay them what I have," Rego responded.

"Nonsense, my friend. It's what Panama is all about, good hospitality. I can show you a little of old Panama before you go. Plus, we can talk to my father, I think he can help you with your ship," Doc said with confidence.

Rego smiled and agreed. He was very happy at his good fortune. Much better than what he had encountered before.

The gang plank was lowered, and the ship's crew began to disembark from the ship. Rego walked behind Doc as they headed to the boardwalk. Several locals stood and waited for the sailors to get off the ship. Most of them were family members, brothers, sisters, parents, all waiting to greet one, or some of the workers getting off the ship.

Rego casually walked down the gang plank, and then spotted some people he did not want to see. Coutier and Gomes stood behind a large post just beyond the end of the walkway. Rego looked around in desperation. There was no way to turn around and go back up to the ship. He had to walk off the gang plank. He was trapped. Coutier spotted him and smiled. He knew he had Rego this time.

Doc paid no attention to the men in the beige overcoats. He walked past them, but Rego stopped as he stepped off the walkway. Doc turned around to see Rego stop as the two men in overcoats stepped in front of him.

"Mr. Ouliveyra, this is where your journey ends," Coutier said with an angry look on his face. "You are coming with us."

Rego felt defeated. He had nowhere else to run, they had him cornered. Doc came walking up behind the two men, "Hey, what's going on here?" he demanded.

Gomes turned towards Doc and put his hand to his face, "Back off, sir, this is no concern of yours."

"Hey, if you're here to arrest this guy, let's see some ID," Doc continued to insist. "I know you guys sure as hell aren't cops. Not from here, you're not!" He pushed Gomes' hand down. Gomes then shoved Doc away, but Doc shoved him right back.

Coutier whipped around with his fist, "What the hell is this? Arrest that man too!" Rego saw that Coutier's head was turned and seized upon the opportunity. With one swing, Rego smashed the satchel against Coutier's head and knocked him backwards. Then he swung it again and smacked Gomes right in the stomach. Gomes doubled over in pain. Rego then swung the satchel one last time, hitting Gomes in the face with an uppercut. Doc jumped on a park bench and whistled loudly in the direction of a group of cars parked along the street. Rego took off running as fast as he could away from the docks. Coutier tried to get up but Doc pushed him down again.

He yelled out to Rego, "Wait!" But it was too late. Rego was gone, running like a madman down the street. Doc took one last look at the agents on the ground and then ran over to a waiting car driven by his brother. He jumped in the front seat and the car sped off.

Coutier and Gomes got to their feet, cursing and swearing. "After him, he doesn't leave this city!" Coutier shouted as they stumbled after Rego.

Rego ran as fast as he could down the foreign streets of Colón. He didn't know where he was going but he kept running. He knocked people down as he ran by. He could hear the shouts of Coutier and Gomes behind him. He turned back quickly as he ran, and he could see the beige coats running far behind him. He turned down one street, then another, changing directions at each turn, trying to shake them. Coutier was determined that he wasn't going to let Rego get away this time. He had come too far now.

Rego ran down an alley, but it was a dead end. He looked for a fire escape to climb, but they were too high. He decided to make a run for it back out to the main street and ran as fast as he could. Just then Coutier and Gomes turned the corner to trap him. Rego panicked but he kept running full speed and plowed right into Coutier, knocking him backwards into the street. Car tires screeched to a halt as the men grappled on the concrete. Rego punched Coutier down with his fist.

"You dirty bastard, leave me *alone*," he screamed at him. Gomes tried to tackle him, but Rego used his quick feet to dodge him. Rego took a swing at him with the satchel again but Gomes ducked. However, he ducked right into another car coming from the other way. The car slammed on its brakes and Gomes dove out of the way, just in time.

Rego took off down the street once again and rounded the corner. He almost reached the next block when a car slammed on its brakes right in front of him. Doc stuck his head out of the window of the car, "Get in!" he yelled. Rego jumped into the back seat of the car and they sped off with Coutier and Gomes stumbling down the street after them.

Rego sprawled out on the back seat, exhausted. "Thank you, thank you," he said over and over again.

"Who the hell were those guys?" Doc yelled at him. "I thought you had never been here before?"

Rego was too exhausted to answer him. He just motioned his hand for the car to keep going forward. Doc's brother sped down the streets and headed for their neighborhood. They pulled into a garage underneath an apartment building and the car came to a stop.

Doc looked back at Rego, who had finally caught his breath. "You'll be safe here, they won't find this place. Trust me," Doc assured him.

Coutier and Gomes made it back to their car where LaBonne was standing, still wearing his neck brace.

"Where is he?" he asked with his hands in the air.

Coutier had a black eye and cut lip. Gomes was holding his stomach and his face had cuts on it as well. The three of them looked like a motley group. All of them had been beaten at their own game by Rego.

"Damn kid," Gomes muttered under his breath.

"Forget him for now," Coutier said wiping his lip with a handkerchief. "We must change our plan now. I know where the little cuss is heading. We can comb this town over and we won't find him. Our only chance is to cut him off at the source." The three men piled into the small car and sped away.

Rego knelt on the floor inside the apartment peering out a window. There was nothing to see except for the other apartment windows across the way. His mind was weary, and he was tired of looking over his shoulder at every turn.

Doc and his brother, Luis, walked in from a small kitchen. Doc handed Rego a small glass of water. "Here, have some water and calm down," he said looking at Rego worried. "They won't find you here, it is safe." He sat down on the couch and Luis stood there staring at Rego. "This is my brother, Luis. My mother is asleep in her room and my father is still at work."

Rego took a sip of water from the glass and looked away from the window. "You guys saved my tail. I don't know how to thank you."

Doc nodded with an assured look on his face, "Like I said, we Panamanians are known for our hospitality. Besides, those guys were not Panamanian police, I knew they were no good." Luis sat down on the arm of the couch, still glaring at Rego. Doc looked up at his brother. They both wanted to know what was going on. "You can stay on the couch as long as you like, my mother won't care. But tell me, who were those guys?"

Rego stared at the glass in his hand and shook his head. "I don't know, but they won't leave me alone." His voice started to shake. He looked at the two brothers on the couch, "I swear I haven't done anything, honest. They just keep following me."

Luis finally broke his silence. "I don't buy it. They want something. That is for sure. Who the hell are you, anyway?"

Doc gave Luis an obvious look. "Let him be. Can't you see he's scared out of his mind? He worked with me on the ship from Lima. He's a friend of mine, relax."

Luis shook his head and got up. "Well, he can't stay here long. We don't need that kind of trouble, whatever the hell it is. Frankly, I don't give a damn who you are or why those men are chasing you. You're putting us all in danger. Papa won't like it, for certain."

The sun had gone down over Colón. The tropical breeze blew in from the sea through the palm trees and papaya leaves. The city had grown quiet in the night hours. With the windows open, the salt and sea air were fresh on the tip of one's nose.

Doc walked over and opened the two windows in the apartment to let in the fresh sea air. His mother, Francesca, was busy in the kitchen preparing dinner. She always wore a smile on her face and was always kind to everyone. Doc helped her in the kitchen, preparing beans on the stove, while Rego cut up vegetables on the counter.

"You are good in the kitchen, Mr. Rego. I like that," Francesca commended him.

"Thank you, Mrs. Vega," he said politely. "I always like helping my grandmother in the kitchen." Rego began to think about his grandmother again. He remembered the times when she was more active, when his grandfather was still living. She would cook large meals on Sunday after Mass and invite as many friends as she could. She would cook salted beef, steamed potatoes, corn and even pastries for dessert. Sometimes at Easter and other special holidays, she would make a yellow cake with frosting on top when she could buy the ingredients. It was his grandfather's favorite. He always liked the Sunday meals she would cook, and he smiled as he thought about her.

As he cut up the vegetables, he asked Doc, "Is there a place that has telephones that I may call my grandmother in Brasilia? I don't want to trouble you with such a long-distance call."

"Oh yes, there is a center downtown that has a bank of telephones for international calling," Doc assured him. "I can take you there tomorrow."

"I have some money that they paid us on the ship. I will use that. Do you think it will be enough for a few minutes?" he asked Doc. "I will spend it all if I have to."

Francesca smiled at him, "What a wonderful gesture. I am sure she would appreciate that."

"It should be enough," Doc said. "The operators can tell you how long you can talk. We will go when they open in the morning."

Just then, Doc's father, Carlos, walked in the door from work. He sat down at the kitchen table and looked very tired. He worked at the loading docks down at the port. Francesca walked over and kissed the top of his head. "I hope you are hungry, I have many helpers tonight. We have a guest."

"Who do we have here, young man?" Carlos asked Rego.

Rego put down his cutting knife and shook Carlos' hand. "I am Rego Ouliveyra, sir. A pleasure to meet you. I worked with Doc on the ship."

Carlos glanced at Doc, "And how was Lima this time, son?"

"Very nice, Papa. Got kind of rough near the end though, didn't it Rego?" Doc said with a sly grin.

"What?" Rego asked in dismay.

Doc slapped him on the shoulder, "You know, the storm that came up." Doc looked his father and said laughing, "He fell from his bunk one night, right on his head." Rego smiled and remembered the knot on the back of his head.

"You found the straps then, didn't you?" Carlos said chuckling. "I remember the first time I hit my head. Don't feel bad."

"Thank you for letting me stay in your home, sir," Rego said to Carlos. "I won't be in the way long."

"A friend of my son is a friend of mine. You are welcome here."

Luis said very little during the meal. He was still very suspicious of the newcomer in their home. He didn't like the idea of strange men chasing this intruder through the streets as if he were a criminal. And now he was in their home. He was worried of the danger Rego might impose on their family.

Doc spoke up at the table, "Papa, Rego is on his way to Greece."

Carlos straightened in his chair, "Ah, the Mediterranean. A man traveling the world, I see." Rego nodded to him as he ate his corn. "I have never been there."

Rego answered, "I am working my way over there. I have always wanted to see it."

"Papa, do you know of any ships that are going across to the Med in the coming days?" Doc asked his father.

Carlos thought for only a few seconds and took a long drink from his bottle of beer. "Many head that way, some cargo, some passenger. But, I do not know their timetables. We can find that out tomorrow for you. Perhaps I know someone that can find you work in the galley on one of them. My son knows others that are stewards as well."

Rego smiled in appreciation, "Thank you, sir. That sounds great to me." Luis frowned at the whole idea. He knew Rego was running, not sightseeing.

Carlos put his hands down on the table. "Tomorrow night, we set up the antenna for the television and we watch the match!" he pronounced. "You do like football, don't you?" he asked Rego.

Rego had all but forgotten about the World Cup. The first match was being played the next evening on opening night in Mexico City. The host country was playing the USSR. "Oh yes, I do very much. I play all the time back home in Brasilia."

"Yes, a wonderful way to spend a Sunday afternoon. Luis and Carlo are very good as well," Carlos said.

"Carlo?" Rego asked curiously.

"Yes, yes, my name is Carlo, just like my Papa," Doc said. "But everybody calls me Doc." Luis and his father both shook their head.

Francesca stood up, "Come, my son they call Doc, help your mother clean this table."

The next morning, Doc and Rego walked down the streets towards the town center of Colón. Rego kept looking over his shoulder at every turn they made.

"Why do you carry that thing everywhere?" Doc asked him, pointing at the satchel around his shoulders.

"I don't know. I just always have. I never leave home without it." Rego said matter-of-factly.

"Well, it looks stupid," Doc said shaking his head. Rego did not care. They approached a large building with many windows. "This is the telephone center. It should be open now."

They walked in and approached the operator counter. Rego took out the money he had been paid on the ship. He counted it to himself and he saw he had about ten balboa. "I would like to call Brasilia, please. Will this be enough?" he asked the woman at the counter.

The woman started to trace her finger down a chart that listed countries and rates. "You may talk for two and a half minutes to Brasilia for nine balboa." She handed him a small index card with a number on it. Rego gave her the money that he had. "Go to booth number seven, dial your number and the operator will put you through."

Doc followed him to the booth, "I will wait over here. I hope you get her on the line." Rego nodded and got inside the booth and closed the door. He dialed the number and waited for the call to be put through.

He heard the line start to ring. It rang two more times, then finally someone picked up the line. "Hello?" a voice said.

"Rosa! Is that you?" Rego asked with excitement.

"Rego? Rego is that you?" Rosa answered. He was very excited to hear her voice.

"Yes. Yes, it's me! You are at Grandma's?"

"Yes. She is with me now. I am helping her go to Mass. I'm going with her. It's so good to hear your voice. Where are you?" she asked curiously.

"Panama. Listen, I can't talk long, I only have a couple minutes. How is she doing?" Rego asked urgently.

"*Panama.* Really?" Rosa was excited to hear his voice and how far he had traveled. "What's it like there? Is it pretty?" She was amazed he had made it that far.

"Rosa, please, they are going to cut me off soon!"

"Alright, alright. Grandma is fine. But Rego, I have to tell you something. Something bad has happened."

"What is it?" he asked expecting the worst.

"It's your uncle, he has passed away. Two days ago," she said with her voice getting softer.

Rego's mind raced. He could only remember one uncle. He had not seen him since he was a little boy. "Uncle Enso? Grandma's brother?"

"Yes."

"Oh no, that is terrible news. How is Grandma taking it?"

"She is alright. But she wants to go to Salvador for his funeral. I wish you were here, I need your help," she said with some frustration, but she knew that Rego had to keep going.

"I'm sorry, Rosa. You know I would be there if I could. Tell Grandma I am thinking of her. Is she there?"

"She's here. But, she is getting ready."

"Tell her I will be home as soon as I can," Rego said, his voice was turning to sadness. He really started to miss them now. A voice came on the line, the operator said he only had one minute left for the call.

"Rosa, I have less than a minute left. Listen, I want to come home, I need to be there with you and Grandma. When are you going to Salvador?"

She cut him off however, saying, "Rego, do you still have the leather case?"

"Yes."

"Have you opened it?"

"No."

"Good, don't open it. Just keep going, ok? You have to do what the man told you to do. Trust me, I know why you are doing this now," she said, speaking as fast as she could.

"Why, what did you find out? Please, tell me!" he shouted into the phone.

"Just do it for Enso, Rego. Do it for his friend Jacomé. I know you can. I'm praying for you," she said sweetly.

"Jacomé? Who is that? What am I supposed to do?" he asked frantically.

"The man who gave you the case. The one who was shot outside the building. Don't worry, Rego. Just keep going, ok? You won't regret it."

"Rosa, wait, what is it that..." Rego looked at the phone in panic. "Hello? Hello?" She was gone. His two and a half minutes were up. His hands trembled as he put the phone back on the hook. He looked desperately in his pockets, but he had no more money. His mind raced through the things she had just said. *What did she mean about Uncle Enso? What was it that she found out?* He sat down on the bench in the booth and sobbed a little. He looked at the satchel and stared at it. The initials on the flap had begun to fade. He stared at the faded letters, ESB, for what seemed like an eternity, then put his head down in his hands and sobbed.

He softly said to himself, "Enso Sanches Botelha." He lifted his head, his eyes red with tears. "How did I not see this?" he said to himself again. "It belongs to my uncle."

Rego stumbled out of the phone booth and walked over to where Doc was sitting. Doc could tell that he looked somewhat rattled.

"Are you ok, kid? Did you get to talk to her?" Doc asked concerned.

"Yes, she was there. It's just been a while since I've seen her, that's all." Rego gathered himself and straightened up. "So, where to now?"

"Let's go meet my father down at the docks. Maybe he found out something about the ships."

Rego looked worried. He didn't like the idea of going down there. He knew the agents were still around looking for him. "Are you sure we should go down there?" he asked. "I don't know. I'm sure those assholes are still hanging around there."

Doc thought about it, "You're right, let's go get my brother's car. We can drive down there, and you can wait in the car." Rego agreed. That did sound much better.

Rego waited in the car and sat low on the front seat and peered over the ledge. Doc walked down the boardwalk to where his father worked. Carlos saw him coming and went out to talk with him. Rego saw him pointing down one way and then another. *Maybe he found something,* Rego thought to himself. Rego looked all around, still keeping an eye out for the agents. They were nowhere to be seen.

A few minutes later, Doc came back to the car and got in. "You're in luck my friend. A passenger ship just came through the canal last night and let off a bunch of people. Father said they are re-loading it today." He started the car and began to drive away. He pointed down the boardwalk, "See that big one rising up over the top of everything? That's it."

Rego pulled himself up and looked over all the smaller ships lining the port and saw a massive ship towering over all of them. Across the stern, it read the name in huge white letters, *MONTENERO.* In smaller letters below the name was written, *España.* Rego couldn't believe the size of the ship. "*That's* a passenger ship?" he asked in amazement.

"Yes," Doc answered. "For all the rich tourists now. They get on these huge ships and sail everywhere. But they also haul cargo as well. Just like the *Titanic*," he said laughing.

"Oh, shit, I hope not like the *Titanic*," Rego said with worry. "How can that thing float?"

"Ah, it can float alright. They build them bigger and bigger all the time now," Doc said.

"Well, where is it going? And when?" Rego asked with intrigue.

"It's leaving in the morning. They will load it up today and passengers will start to board tonight. But they are not cleared to disembark until the morning though, probably around six a.m.," Doc said. He looked over at Rego and told him what he wanted to hear. "It's going across the Atlantic. The ship is based in Spain. First it will stop somewhere in the Lesser Antilles, then it will head for the Straits of Gibraltar. Then, on to good old Greece, my friend."

Rego smiled and shook his head in amazement. "Doc, you are good, my friend. You are very good. I can't believe it. How can I find work on the ship?"

"I will make a call to a friend of mine who routinely works as an assistant steward on the passenger ships up and down the coast of Peru and Columbia. I will see what he can do." Rego leaned back in his seat with relief. He couldn't believe it was going to be this easy. He just hoped the ship was going to make a stop in Malta. If not, then Greece would be close enough for him.

They made it back to the apartment and Rego plopped down on the couch. Doc walked into the kitchen where the phone was sitting. Rego looked at the satchel and the initials on it. He felt sad about hearing of his uncle's death. He knew that his health had been failing, but it always seems to happen when you least expect it. *Why did Enso give me this case?* he asked himself in his

104

mind over and over again. *And why were these agents after me? Why did they kill Jacomé? What could be worth killing a man for?* His mind ached over all these questions. The suspense was too much for him to bear. He had to open the case and see what was inside. He put the case on his lap and started to undo the clasp. His forehead began to bead with sweat.

"Good news, my friend!" Doc said bouncing into the sitting room. Rego was startled back into comprehension. He set the case down by his feet.

"What did you find out?" he asked wiping the sweat from his forehead.

"My friend said they are always looking for help in the galleys on the large ships. All you need is to show up on time and most importantly, have a clean uniform," Doc told him.

Rego looked at his clothes, they were all worn and dirty. "I don't think this will do. Can you buy them somewhere?"

Doc had a sly grin on his face. "You can, but it would take weeks for you to get one." His lifted his eyebrow slightly. "Or you can borrow one of mine."

Rego sat up on the couch, "Don't tell me you have a uniform too?"

"Of course. I am a steward, so is Luis. I have three of them myself," Doc said proudly. "Hell, if I were as daring as you, I'd go on one of those long voyages too!" He walked into the room he shared with Luis and then came out with white uniform with black trousers. "We're about the same size, try it on."

Rego put on the uniform and it fit him fairly well. "Doc, I don't know how to thank you. You've done all these kind things for me. How can I ever repay you?"

Doc shrugged his shoulders, "Don't worry about it, I don't need three of those things anyway. My mother always likes to get us new ones." Doc was glad that he could help Rego. "Hey, if it was me and I was in a jam in Brasilia, I know you would do the same for me." Rego nodded and shook his hand.

Rego helped Francesca clean the kitchen after dinner. She enjoyed his company and loved the way he helped around the house so much. He felt he should help her as much as he could since they were being so kind to him.

Carlos and Luis worked feverishly on the television, trying to tune in the only station in Panama. Carlos turned the knobs and held up the wires on the back. He yelled out the open window next to the TV, "Luis, move it around some more!"

Luis was on the roof, just above the window adjusting a small antenna. "Now try it!" he yelled back.

A picture started to come into focus on the small black and white screen. "A little more, a little more! Steady it now. There, right there!" Carlos yelled excitedly up to Luis. "I found the match, it is about to begin!"

All five of them gathered around to watch the small TV. The match between Mexico and the USSR was about to begin to start the World Cup. Carlos, Luis, and Francesca sat on the couch while Doc sat on the floor close to the TV. Rego sat on one of the wooden chairs from the kitchen. He was so excited he was getting to see one of the matches. He wished he was there to see it in person.

"Brazil plays their first match on Wednesday," Rego said staring at the screen intently.

Carlos nodded from the couch, "Pelé, his squad looks good this year. I like their chances. I know you are proud of them." Rego nodded.

"Who do you like this year, sir?" Rego asked him.

"I always hope for Mexico, and I am glad they are the host this year. It is a big moment for all Mexicans. And of course, our brothers in Peru. But the West Germans, they will be a tough squad to beat this year. The Europeans know the game well." Luis and Doc both nodded in agreement.

"Shhh, quiet," Francesca said. "I can't hear." She liked to watch the matches just as much as the men did.

They watched the match and reacted to every play on the goal. There were many close calls at the goals but neither team could get the ball into the nets. Two hours later, the match was over, and it ended in a draw.

Doc stood in front of the TV, pointing his hand toward it in frustration. "Can you believe that? No goals at all. It ended in a lousy draw!"

Carlos quickly corrected him, "A tie is not bad for Mexico. The Soviets are a tough team to draw in the opening round. I am proud of the Mexicans. They played well." He looked at the old clock on the wall, it was almost eleven.

Francesca spoke up for Rego. "We should let this young man get his rest and give him his bed. He has a long trip ahead of him."

"Thank you, Mrs. Vega. I won't forget how kind everyone has been to me." Rego knew he was very fortunate to have found these people. They turned off the TV and they all went to bed. Rego flopped down on the couch and was asleep in no time.

Chapter 11

The clock ticked on the wall. It was just a few minutes before four a.m. when a hand picked up the satchel sitting at the end of the couch. Quietly the dark figure opened the clasp on the satchel and pulled out the contents. He flipped through the small stack of papers, examining each one closely by the dim light coming from the window. Rego stirred on the couch and turned over onto his side. The dark figure quickly slid the papers back into the satchel and then walked over to the kitchen chair, still sitting near the TV. He turned and faced it to the couch. The sound of the creaking wooden chair awakened Rego. He pulled the chain on the small lamp next to the couch and sat up on his elbow. He looked towards the chair to see Luis.

"Interesting little case you have here," Luis said very smartly, sitting on the chair with the satchel on his lap. Rego stared at him with suspicion and disbelief. "Now I see why you are such a popular guy. I think it's time you and me had a little chat."

Rego slowly sat up on the couch. "I've got nothing to say to you. Give that back to me, it's mine."

Luis knew he had Rego now. His suspicions had been confirmed. "Now I see why those government men were after you. They're agents, aren't they?" he said cleverly.

"I don't care who they are, they mean nothing to me. Now give that back to me!" Rego grew more impatient.

"Do you really think I'm going to let you out of here with this? No way, kid. This little jewel is coming with me down to the authorities," he said as he stood up. "I'm not going to let you bring all this trouble into *my* family's home."

"Oh no, it's not!" Rego jumped off the couch and reached for the satchel. He struggled with Luis, but he could not pry it from his hands. Luis shoved him down to the couch.

"What's going on in here?" Carlos demanded as he came from his room.

"Nothing, Papa. Rego was just leaving for his ship," he said hiding the satchel behind his back.

"He's lying! He is trying to steal my stuff," Rego protested, throwing on his clothes. He picked up his jacket and the uniform Doc had given him.

"Is this true, Luis? What are you taking from him?" Carlos insisted.

"He's hiding secrets from his own government. I saw it with my own eyes. He's putting us all in danger, and I won't stand it for it! He's been staying here, a perfect stranger, taking advantage of us, acting as if everything is fine. But Carlo and I know what's going on. He's running from his government and he's hiding secrets from them!" Luis yelled.

Rego ran behind Luis and snatched the case from his hands. Francesca and Doc came out into the sitting room to see what was going on. "I'm not hiding anything," Rego insisted. "This belongs to my uncle, it is *his* business. I am only delivering it for him." His voice was shaking. He wanted out of there as soon as possible. "I won't trouble you anymore. Or *you* either," he snarled at Luis.

"You're not going anywhere, punk," Luis snarled as he grabbed his arm.

"Let him go," Carlos said sternly. Luis immediately released his arm. "His business is none of ours. You go do what you need to do," he said to Rego. "He is wishing to go in peace and we will let him."

Rego looked at Francesca and Doc apologetically. "I will never forget your kindness. I thank you." He took one last stern look at Luis and turned and walked out the door.

Rego rushed down the stairwell and dashed out of the building and down the street. He ran all the way down the darkened streets to the port. The port was brightly lit and busy with workers. He found an old public bathroom just outside the port and went inside to change into the uniform. He stuffed his old clothes into the satchel, paying little attention to the papers inside. He didn't care what Luis had found. He was going to honor what his uncle had requested, no matter what.

He stepped out of the bathroom wearing the white uniform and black trousers. He walked down the busy boardwalk to the *Montenero*. Rego was amazed at the incredible size of the ship as he walked closer. It was much larger than the last ship he was on from Peru. He spotted the walkway that led to the main deck of the ship. He climbed his way to the main deck where a man in uniform stood with a clipboard.

"Sir, you are the first mate?" Rego said with confidence.

"That I am, and who might you be?" the first mate asked.

"Rego Ouliveyra, sir. I am reporting for duty in the galley. Sorry I am late."

The first mate looked him over and stared at his uniform. "ID, please," the man said in a tired voice. Rego dug into the pockets of his jacket and pulled out his identification papers and handed them to the man. The man flipped through the papers quickly and then handed them back. "Crew cabins are on D and E deck. Stow your gear and report to the galley on E deck immediately. You will be on time, from now on, mister!" He stepped aside and let Rego come aboard.

Rego found the stairs that led to each deck. He couldn't help but notice how nice the ship was. It was decorated very ornately and stylishly. The walls were covered with decorative wallpaper and trimmed with polished wood. All the handrails on the steps were polished wood as well. The walls in the stairwell were clean and white and the steps were bright red and lined with shiny metal strips. The *Montenero* was completely different from the drab cargo ship he had sailed on from Lima. He smiled at his good fortune. He was happy to be on this ship and was eager to find out what his duties would be. He knew the nice uniform he had been given was his ticket away from the mop and bucket.

It was almost a quarter past five a.m. when Rego came upon a door on E deck that read *COCINA*. He pushed the double doors open and found the kitchen to be electric with activity. People were rushing around everywhere preparing breakfast for the ships new passengers who had just come aboard a few hours earlier in the night. The room was full of stainless-steel counters, sink tops, large white refrigerator and freezer doors and black stoves. Kitchen utensils, pots, pans and a variety of other mixing tools, hung from stainless steel racks on the ceiling. It was worlds away from the kitchen Rego saw on the ship from Lima. Workers rushed around Rego who was standing just inside the doorway. Some bumped into him without even batting an eye at him and rushed past.

"What are you doing just standing around?" a firm voice boomed from behind him. Rego quickly turned around to see the kitchen manager and head steward, Hector, standing over him. He was easily a foot taller than Rego. He had dusty blonde hair and thin wire glasses on. He spoke in an accent Rego hadn't heard before, but still in clear enough Spanish that he understood.

Rego straightened up his posture and tried to speak over all the clatter. "I am Rego Ouliveyra. I arrived late, sir, but I am reporting for galley duty."

"I'm Hector Van der Berg. I'm the head honcho around here. From now on, you report for duty at four-thirty every morning for breakfast detail and four p.m. each afternoon for dinner detail. Got that?" Hector ordered as he strolled through the kitchen, inspecting each area. Rego nodded quickly and tried to keep up. "I'll put you on tray and table detail since you are new. We have a small breakfast offering before the set-sail festivities on the Main deck. Is this your gear?" Hector pointed towards his jacket and satchel. Rego quickly nodded again. "Get it out of here. The kitchen crew barracks are down that hall and to the left," Hector said pointing towards a small door in the back of the kitchen. "Be back here in five minutes!"

Rego quickly walked through the small door and down the narrow hallway and followed the signs above his head to the crew cabins down the hallway. He had no idea which door to open. The hallway was lined with at least twenty doors, one for each cabin. He slowed his pace in the hallway and looked at each door. They were all the same. He finally decided to knock on one of the doors with the number eleven on it. He waited for a few seconds, but no one answered. He slowly pulled on the door handle and opened the door slightly.

"You coming in or not?" a muffled voice said from inside the cabin. Rego slowly peered around the door and into the dimly lit cabin. A figure lying on a bunk covered with several blankets, briefly lifted his head. He took a quick glance at Rego and turned over to face the wall again. "Great, another new guy," he said sleepily.

Rego looked around the small cabin. There was another bunk above the sleeping man and two small lockers beside them. He turned to his right and saw another single bunk along the inside wall with a small locker next to it as well. The locker had a key stuck in the keyhole with a thick strand of string hanging from the key. A small mirror hung on the far-right wall and one chair in the corner. "Are any of these bunks free?" Rego asked shyly, not wanting to disturb the man in the bunk.

The sleeping man lifted his hand from underneath the blankets and pointed towards the single bunk on the inside wall, "That one is," he said without looking up. "Knock yourself out."

Rego put his things down on the bunk and looked at the locker. "I can use this locker here?" he asked again.

The man in the bunk rolled over finally to look at Rego. He looked at him like he was a madman. "*Yes*, use it!" He sat up on his elbow and realized he was being a jerk. "Sorry, man. I was out all night in Colón and my head is killing me. I'm Bolo," he said reaching his hand out. "Keep the key with you, it locks when you turn it and then you just pull it out."

"Rego," he said shaking Bolo's hand. He knelt down in front of the locker and examined how it worked.

"I don't go on duty until ten. I work lunch and the midnight cabin detail. Is Van der Berg riding everyone's ass yet?" he asked as he rolled over on his back.

Rego immediately remembered he had to be back in the kitchen right away. "Damn, I forgot I have to get back. I'll let you sleep. Sorry for waking you." He quickly threw his jacket and the satchel into the locker and turned the key. The key slid out and he looked at the thick string dangling from the key. It finally dawned on him to wear it around his neck. He stared at the key for a few seconds, then down at the locker. It was the first time he had put the satchel down to leave it behind. He knew it would be safe in the locker though. He threw the key around his neck and stuffed it under his white uniform. "See you, Bolo," he said and dashed out of the room.

Rego walked back into the busy kitchen. He wondered where he should go for the tray and table detail. It didn't take him long to find out though. As he walked through the kitchen, he saw large stainless-steel serving trays being loaded with eggs, potatoes, fruit and a variety of other dishes, and carried through another set of double doors on the other side of the kitchen. One by one, they were being carried out. Rego stood in line and picked up a tray of potatoes and followed the person in front of him out of the kitchen. He immediately saw the fancy dining room lined with tables with white linen tablecloths, clean glasses and rolled up napkins containing eating utensils. The ceiling was decorated with finely ornate chandeliers and the floor was nicely carpeted. The white-clothed tables were surrounded with chairs that were perfectly polished. Rego couldn't believe his eyes as he took in the sight of everything. He stepped over to the buffet line and placed the steam tray into a slot next to the tray full of eggs.

He soon learned that passengers would start entering at six a.m. for breakfast. He was amazed at how much detail and effort was put forth for the morning meal and the ship hadn't even left the port yet. The food smelled wonderful to Rego and he was aching to take a break and eat some of it, but he resisted and continued to carry the trays out.

He paid attention to other workers to see what he should do next after the buffet line was set. Over by the far wall of the dining room, some of his co-workers were lining up against the wall and stood motionless with their hands behind their backs. Rego decided to walk over and stand with them. He glanced over at the tall, slender man standing next to him. The room was empty, but all the workers stood against the wall, saying nothing.

The tall man finally broke his silence and said, "You're new here, aren't you?" still looking forward. It was a language Rego had never heard before.

Rego glanced at him, not understanding. "Hm?" he asked.

The slender man then spoke in broken Spanish, "New here?"

"Oh, yes, I am."

"I'm Lars, from Holland. Sorry, my Spanish is not so good," Lars said quietly.

"Rego, glad to meet you. I'm from Brasilia," Rego whispered back.

"Sorry, my Portuguese is even worse than my Spanish," he whispered, trying not to be noticed. Rego shrugged his shoulders. "Never talk to the passengers in the dining area. Just pick up the plates when they are done. Fill the glasses with water if they are less than half full. No problem, right?" Rego nodded to him. "This will be a quick meal, a good one to learn on, no? They will want to get to the party outside when we set sail."

114

One of the girls standing in line put her finger to her lips and said, "Shh!" Lars stopped talking and he and Rego stood against the wall and waited for the dining room doors to open.

The clock hanging above the dining room doors read six o'clock exactly. The doors were opened by two attendants in black jacket suits. Soon, a few passengers began to file in the dining room towards the buffet line. As time went on, more and more passengers began to file in. The room looked as though it could hold hundreds of passengers, for it was the main dining room. The noise level in the hall began to rise as more and more people came in for the morning meal. The dining room attendants, one by one, began to leave the wall and take plates and glasses away and walk them back to the kitchen clean-up window. Others walked around with pitchers full of water, filling glasses when they saw them less than half-full. Others carried hot pots of coffee, refilling cups for the coffee drinkers. All of them worked without saying a word, only nodding yes to the passenger's requests. When there were no plates to take away or glasses to refill, they returned to the wall and waited for more. Once a party left their table, another set of workers came behind them and reset the table with fresh linens and dinnerware. It was a very efficiently run show.

Rego got the hang of the job right away. He didn't know if he liked waiting on the elite passengers, but he was certain he liked it much better than mopping.

Soon, the last of the passengers started to leave the dining hall. Breakfast ended early, just after seven, due to the passengers wanting to get to the main and promenade decks to take part in the send-off party. Other attendants began to leave the wall and slowly pick up the plates and glasses from all the tables. After the passengers had left, a more casual atmosphere descended upon the workers. Some began to talk with one another as they worked. Rego stacked some plates and glasses and carried them over to the wash window. Lars came up behind him with his hands full too.

"Not bad for a dry run, eh Rego?" he asked in his broken Spanish.

Rego nodded back to him, "Not bad. Man, I have never seen so much food."

"You get used to it. It costs a pretty penny for these hotshots to travel like this, and of course, not a penny is spared on the food," Lars said going back for more dishes. "We'll get to eat after we clear off all these tables. We have our own tables in the kitchen area."

Rego was glad to hear that. He had worked up an appetite running around to all the tables, while he watched the passengers eat the delicious looking food. He put down another stack of plates at the window. "Do we get to watch the ship set sail?" he asked curiously. He was eager to see the festivities when the ship pulled away. He thought about old movies he had seen, watching happy travelers pull away on crowded ships, throwing streamers down to the docks, yelling and cheering and waving goodbye to people below.

"Yes, but you have to change into civilian clothes. And, you can only watch from the promenade deck. On the send-offs and the main deck parties, we are not allowed on the main deck," Lars instructed him.

"Are you going up?" Rego asked him.

"Nah, I've seen my share of send-offs. You go ahead," Lars replied.

Rego was so excited about watching the ship set sail, he totally forgot about his hunger and skipped the morning meal with his co-workers. He did not have to work during lunch, so he figured he would grab a bite to eat then. He really didn't want to eat that much food anyway. He couldn't believe the amounts of food that were brought out for just one meal.

He threw on his old clothes and tried to pat his hair down as best as he could. He casually walked up to H deck, which was the promenade deck, and made his way over to the starboard side and found a spot on the rail. The decks were wide, and the wood floors were spotless. He smiled and shook his head and thought to himself, *I pity the poor bastard who has to clean these decks.* He felt vastly underdressed compared to the mobs of passengers milling around on the deck, but he tried to keep a low profile and tried to find a nice spot tucked away from the crowds. He stood near the rail very close to the stern. He could see the vast length of the ship and could barely make out the bow way down at the other end of the dock. He could hear the steam venting from the stacks above but could not see them. The best view was obviously from the main deck, but he knew he would get up there soon enough.

The crowds began to gather close to the starboard rail and started to cheer when the whistle blew from the main stack on top of the ship. Confetti and streamers began to sail from the decks above and below and they cheered wildly when the ship began to pull away from the dock. Rego stared at the scene in amazement. It was just as he had seen in the American movies in the old movie houses with Rosa. He sorely wished Rosa was here with him to witness this wonderful event. His heart began to feel sadness as the passengers cheered their departure. He thought about his poor grandmother mourning the death of her brother. He yearned to be with her and comfort her, but Rego also thought of his uncle and the quest he had mysteriously sent him on. He wondered what it all meant and why Rosa insisted that he continue onward. He looked up at the mighty ship that started to carry him to his destination. *I'm finally on my way,* he thought. He nodded to himself in disbelief, as a single tear ran down his face.

Chapter 12

Rego went back to the cabin and decided to rest for a while. He had slept very little after the football match and his early and unexpectedly hasty departure from the apartment. He walked in to find Bolo still trying to get some sleep and his other roommate standing in front of the mirror, trying to perfect his hair.

"Hey, there's the new guy. I saw you busing tables earlier. Welcome aboard, I'm Erik," he said very chipper.

"I'm Rego," he answered, shaking his hand.

"We didn't have anybody on that bunk the whole last leg," Erik said still staring in the mirror. "Glad you made it. The more the merrier, I say. Right Boly old boy?" he said, throwing a towel at Bolo's head.

"Leave me alone and stop calling me that," Bolo protested and turned his back to them.

Rego sat on his bunk, which had fresh linens folded up and sitting on the pillow. "Erik, your accent is much like another guy I met standing in the line. His name was Lars. Are you from Holland too?"

Erik laughed. "Yeah, Lars and I are from the same school. We are here on a work-study program from the local university in Rotterdam. If you can learn Spanish, you can apply to work on these ships for a year and travel the world. That blowhard in the kitchen, Van der Berg, he's from Holland too, unfortunately. He made permanent this past year and quit his studies."

"Where are you from, Bolo?" Rego asked him.

Bolo rolled over again and began to speak in Portuguese. "I am from Lisbon. I can tell you are from my country as well, no?"

"Well, actually I am from Brazil," Rego said, answering him in his native language.

"Alright, no fair. I don't know what the hell you guys are saying," Erik complained.

"I've studied much about the old country," Rego said. "I've always wanted to see it. I think my aunt had the opportunity to go there once. My grandmother said my aunt went on a pilgrimage to Fátima one year."

Bolo sat way up on his bunk now, he loved talking about his home country. "Yes, a wonderful little town. It is a very holy place for all the Portuguese. You should go see it someday."

Erik's frustration grew ever more. He sat down on the lone chair in the corner. "Damnit! I don't understand a word of that gibberish. And my Spanish sucks. Hey, Rego, are you a football fan?"

"Oh yes, I was able to watch the first match last night. Mexico played well." Rego answered him, switching back to Spanish.

"I was so bummed when Holland failed to qualify. But those wankers in Belgium made it. I don't know who the hell I am pulling for now," he said grimly. "But I love to watch the matches."

All three of them agreed on that point. Rego spoke up, "Hey, this ship is so fancy, do you think we might be able to watch some of the matches while we sail?"

Bolo shook his head, "Not out in the middle of nowhere. Not even with the radio we have in the crew area. Only if we are near a country somewhere that we can pick up a signal."

Rego found that disappointing. He knew he wouldn't miss a match if he were at home, but the experience of going on such a long journey was an exceptional excuse. Missing the World Cup matches wouldn't be so bad, he thought. Just then, for the first time, he thought about how long it would actually take to sail the Atlantic.

"Do you guys know how long it will take for us to sail to the Med?" Rego asked.

Erik was back in front of the mirror again, "Around seven to ten days, depending on the seas. There is a map on the main deck that shows the estimated timetable and the ports of call that we will make. Go check it out when you get a chance."

"I will. So, you are on the same shifts as I am?" Rego asked curiously.

Erik looked at him through the mirror, "Yeah, I drew the damn breakfast shift this time around and the lousy dinner schedule. It's not so bad, but those early mornings are a killer, and those meals are busy as hell. Bunch of pigs," he said combing through his dusty blonde locks.

"These are rich passengers, aren't they?" Rego said.

Erik shook his head in disgust. "It's incredible the money running around on this ship. And the strange behavior they have. This one lady used about twenty forks this morning."

Rego started thinking about his first experience on the job this morning. "I saw one lady with a strange hat, feeding her dog that rode around in a handbag! A dog, can you believe that?"

Both of his roommates laughed. "But you should see the women on this ship, man," Erik drawled.

Rego lifted his eyebrow, "Oh yeah?"

"Absolutely. Passengers, even some of the girls we work with. They love my accent. You should come to the crew get-togethers in the break room at night. It's a blast." He stood there and kept combing his hair over and over again. "On my off time, I cruise the decks to check out all the fresh action, and let them gaze upon, Sir Erik," he boasted, admiring the finished product in the mirror.

Bolo and Rego both shook their heads and smiled. "He's loco," Bolo said crawling out of his bunk. "I have to get ready for my shift."

Rego stared at his bunk. "I can't sleep now. I think I'm going to check out the rest of the ship."

Erik glanced at him and said, "Hey, don't go out there like that, my friend. All those rich folks will think you are a stowaway."

120

Rego looked down at his old clothes and then back at Erik with a big frown. He wanted to punch him.

"Here, you can borrow a couple of my shirts," he said, throwing a couple at him. Rego caught them and looked at the shirts with disillusionment. "Go ahead, you'll blend right in."

Rego shook his head and pulled his old shirt off and put one of the borrowed ones on. "Thanks, I'll see you guys later," Rego said and walked out of the room.

The sun was shining brightly on the main deck and many people were out and about. Some strolled slowly around the main walkway that circled the entire ship. Others lay on wooden deck chairs reading books, chatting, and napping in the sun. Other ladies walked their small dogs on the deck with an attendant following behind them carrying a waste container. Rego shook his head in disbelief. "Incredible," he said to himself. A few men played a game with long poles that Rego had never seen before. They pushed discs across the deck floor with the poles, down to a game board with numbers, several yards away. He soon learned the game was called shuffleboard. He stood and watched for a while as the men played.

He walked over to a railing and leaned against it with the sun in his face. He liked the way the warmth felt. It calmed his rattled nerves and made him forget about the awful men that met him at every turn. He thought about Rosa, and how she would love to see this ship. He knew foreign travel interested her and how she had always dreamed of going abroad.

He looked at the massive stack rising from the ship with smoke and steam rising out of it. The massive size of the entire ship astounded him. And since it was such a large ship, it sliced right through the waves, hardly rocking at all as she sailed along. After a while, he turned around to look at the water. He couldn't even guess how high the ship was. The water of the Caribbean, it was a color he had never imagined before. It was a bright, crystal blue, and one could see below the surface very easily. He watched as dolphins swam at the tip of the bow, racing along with the ship. They were so clear in the light blue water. He stood and rested his chin on his hands and just continued to stare at the blue sea.

"It's beautiful, isn't it?" a sweet-sounding voice asked.

Startled, Rego looked up and to find a young girl, no more than twenty, standing next to him. "Que?" he asked, straightening up.

"Oh, I'm sorry," she said. "Do you speak English?"

Rego shook his head and smiled at her, "No, no hablo Ingleis." Her hair was light brown and long and straight, just past her shoulders. Rego thought she was quite pretty. She smiled at him with small thin, red lips. He tried not to stare at her and looked away back at the water. He hadn't spoken to a young, beautiful girl in a long time, it seemed.

"That's ok, my Spanish is not too good either. I'm Lindsey," she said extending her hand.

Rego shook her hand, "Rego."

"Oh, I like that name," she said and leaned against the rail and stared at the water with him.

Rego tried his best to talk to her. "You, um, Americano?" he asked in broken English.

"No, I'm from New Zealand." Rego nodded at her. "I'm a hostess for all the English-speaking passengers. Brits, Aussies, Americans, you name it," she said. "I love to travel, and I love people."

Rego turned and extended his arm outward, offering to walk with her. "Oh sure!" she exclaimed. "I love this sea air, it's so invigorating." Rego smiled politely to her as they walked along the main deck.

She sure does talk a lot, he thought. He had no idea what she was saying most of the time, but she was good company.

"This ship has been around the world, it seems," she said. "I came aboard in New Zealand. I was so lucky to get the job. I couldn't believe it. The trip over on the Pacific was amazing. I loved going through those canals, so fascinating. I noticed you earlier in the crew hallway. What part of the ship do you work in?" Rego looked at her with a clueless expression. He shook his head.

"Work? You, on the ship?" she tried again.

"Ah," he nodded finally in understanding. "La cocina."

"Oh, that's so neat!" she said excitedly. "I bet you are a great cook."

He smiled and chuckled to himself as they continued walking on. They decided to go inside the main gathering area of I deck. There were paintings all along the walls, smoking chairs, leather sofas and rockers for the passengers to lounge in. The light fixtures along the wall were silver with decorative bulbs in each holder. Soon, they came upon a large map of the Caribbean, Atlantic and the Mediterranean. It had a dotted line drawn on it indicating the intended route of the ship from Panama, all the way to Athens. The map had various maritime coordinates at each stop and was marked precisely with each longitude and latitude line.

The two stared at the map and the route of their ship. Lindsey pointed to the route and traced her finger along the dotted line, "These are all the places where we will stop. Here's Panama, then Montserrat, and all the way over to Gibraltar, Malta, Crete, and then Athens." She nodded in anticipation. "Athens. I can't wait to see it. Can you?"

Rego stepped closer to the map and pointed at it. "Malta?" he asked.

"Oh, yes," she responded. "I'm very curious about that one, too. It's the hidden jewel of the Mediterranean. I here it is covered with ancient ruins and many other beautiful things. Did you know that they speak English there? Amazing isn't it? I should fit right in. Sometimes we get to disembark at the ports and do some sightseeing before we head back to sea. I love to shop around in the local markets." She looked at her watch. "Hey, I better go, my shift is about to start. I hope to see you around, Rego." He nodded to her and watched as she walked away.

Rego was never so relieved in all his life. Now he was certain that the ship would be making a stop directly at his destination and he wouldn't have to find another way to Malta. He looked back at the map and stared at the small shape indicating the Maltese Islands. He shook his head at the distance it was from where they were currently. Regardless of how far it was, he breathed easier knowing the *Montenero* was headed for Malta. Just then, Erik came striding up alongside him.

"Why you, sly *dog*," he said cleverly. "Already picking up on Lindsey," he said watching her walk away. Rego rolled his eyes at him and turned from the map.

"She's a fox, that one," Erik said, still watching her.

"Ah, she's alright," Rego said embarrassed. "She just came right up to me, that's all."

"Working that old Brazilian charm, eh? Very nice, my friend." Erik said poking him with his elbow.

Rego laughed. "Yeah, what can I say? Maybe it's the shirt. I didn't understand a damn thing she said though, but she kept talking."

"Yeah, she's into *you*, buddy," Erik kept prodding him. He looked at the clock hanging across the way on the wall. "We better get down to the kitchen, Romeo, or else Hector will blow a gasket." They made their way to the stairwell that led to the kitchen deck. "Maybe you'll see your girlfriend again."

"Shut up," Rego retorted.

Down in the dining room, the tables were being set for the first dinner at sea. Fresh seafood and vegetables and the finest wines and liquors were being prepared. Lars slowly placed dinnerware and empty glasses at each table. Rego followed his lead and did the exact routine at the other tables.

"So many forks," Rego said under his breath.

Lars agreed, "Yeah, as if they need more than one. Or to eat again, for that matter. The evening dinner is the big one. Lots of food and the booze keeps flowing."

"Really?" Rego asked. "What I wouldn't do to have a beer right about now."

"Forget it," Lars responded. "Hector won't let us drink at all the entire time we are on the ship. Only in port. But that goes for the whole crew, not just us. If you get caught, they kick you off at the next port."

Rego tilted his head to one side, "Well, then you can drink all you want once they kick you off." Lars laughed at him.

They worked for over an hour setting all the tables, filing all the pitchers with water, setting out small trays of butter, and folding clean white napkins into nice triangles at each place setting. It was tedious work but Rego picked it up quickly, still gladly favoring it over his last job.

At five minutes to six, the attendants stood along the far wall in a straight line and waited for the double doors to open. Hector walked around the dining room and inspected all the tables. The servers stood behind the buffet line with starched white chef hats on. At exactly six p.m., the doors swung open and a flood of finely dressed passengers began to stream into the dining room. The chatter grew louder and the servers and attendants quietly worked their way around the room attending to the passenger's every need. The dining room personnel did their jobs like a well-oiled machine. If a glass was less than half full, a waiter would glide in unnoticed to refill it. Empty bread baskets were replaced with new ones without anyone lifting a finger to ask for more. Hector stood near the kitchen door observing his crew as they worked stealthily amongst the passengers with grace and promptness. He nodded in approval of their fine work.

Rego blended in effortlessly with his co-workers, removing plates, refilling glasses and serving tea and coffee. Soon each worker had their own section of tables that they attended to and stuck with this notion throughout the journey. Hector liked how they divided the work without being told, as long as the sections had equal amounts of responsibility.

One of the tables in Rego's section was a boisterous crowd of American tourists. Three couples in their forties and fifties sat around the table laughing and joking and sipping on glasses of red wine. There was also a seventh person at the table enjoying the conversation. It was a man with a darker complexion and wore a priest collar and black button-down shirt and trousers. All of them spoke in English but he noticed the priest spoke with an accent. The ladies laughed with raucous enthusiasm at every word that was spoken it seemed. The more wine they drank, the louder they became. The priest would smile in amusement and make light conversation. He obviously knew the passengers well, but sat quietly for the most part, enjoying the meal and laughing at times at his companion's antics. The priest was the only one who acknowledged Rego's presence when he came around to refill the wine and water glasses. He caught Rego's attention each time he refilled his glass of water. The priest would turn his head away from the conversation to say thank you each time. Rego would nod with a slight smile, not saying anything in response.

As the evening wore down, the chatter began to fade, and the people started to get up from their tables and head to other sections of the ship for cigars and brandy and piano music. The table of Americans clumsily started to get up and leave, laughing the whole way out of the dining room. Rego held the chairs out for the ladies as they left the table. As they walked away, the priest stopped and turned to walk over to Rego and put his hand on his shoulder. Rego was surprised to see him stop and speak to him.

"Señor," he said in perfect Spanish. "Soy Padre Juan. Gracias," and shook Rego's hand.

"De nada, Padre," Rego said very softly to the priest. The priest smiled and nodded to him, then walked out of the dining room.

As the days went by, Rego would walk around the decks of the ship, watching all the activity around him. He watched the people play shuffleboard and ping-pong. There were reading rooms inside the ship where people sat with old newspapers and novels and rooms setup with card tables for games such as bridge and gin. There were a variety of ways for the passengers to pass the time as the ship made its way east.

The sea became rougher as they approached the Lesser Antilles in the middle of the week. The sun was mostly hidden by the increasing amount of clouds in the sky and fewer people were out on the decks as the winds picked up. Rego remembered it was Wednesday, the day of the first match in the World Cup for Brazil. He wished he could watch the game or even hear it on the radio, but it was not possible so far away from land.

He walked into his cabin to see Erik in front of the mirror again. "Big party tonight, my friend," Erik said to Rego through the mirror. "Get your section done early tonight and meet us in the crew area. There will be music and dancing."

Rego sat on his bunk and said in a tired voice, "That sounds good. Kind of rough today, isn't it?"

"Yeah, you get used to it. Doesn't bother me," he said flicking his hair back. "But it should make it interesting in the dining room. I can see Hector going insane if glasses start hitting the floor. Won't be the first time." Rego lay down on his bunk. He wasn't too eager to go back to work. "Better get ready, big guy,"

Erik warned him. "Don't be late tonight. Hector almost jumped our ass this morning for coming in two minutes late."

"Yeah, yeah, I'm coming," Rego said yawning. The long hours on his feet were starting to take their toll on him.

"Remember, after work, in the crew area. It's party time," Erik said as he walked out of the cabin.

Rego knelt on the floor in front of the locker and pulled the key from his shirt. He pulled the string necklace over his head and unlocked the locker. He reached in and slid the leather satchel out and stared at it. He looked at the faded letters on the flap that read 'ESB'. He rubbed his tired eyes and stared at the case and thought back to the night he encountered Jacomé. *Why would Uncle Enso ask me to travel so far? What was in this case that would make him ask me to do this?* He had no answer to his questions. He wanted look inside, but he remembered what Jacomé told him just before he died. Rosa had told him not to open it, too. He was so tired and only wished he could be back home again. He shook his head, feeling very hopeless and distraught, then slowly slid the case back into the locker and locked it back.

He made it to the dining room just in time and started preparing the tables. The ship was rocking easily now from side to side as the weather outside continued to worsen. He tried hard to keep his footing as he moved in between the tables, placing the dinnerware and stemware all around each setting. All the workers had a hard time maneuvering around. As the steam trays were carried in, a nervous looking Hector stood nearby, talking rapidly with his assistant.

"The waves may only get worse," he said. "We need everyone to use the utmost caution tonight. Nothing breaks tonight, you hear me?" The assistant nodded and dashed off.

The doors opened, and the crowd streamed in for yet another first-class meal. The laughing Americans sat around their usual table. Some of them stumbled around the chairs as they tried to sit down.

"Gee, I hope they skip the soup tonight!" joked one of the men. His name was Sammy.

"Yes, I will need a much larger glass for my chardonnay tonight, or else I may be wearing it," his wife Alice said with a laugh.

Rego held the chairs out for all the ladies to sit down. Fr. John and the other men waited for them to be seated.

"Good evening, sir," Fr. John said graciously to Rego. "How are you this fine blustery night?"

"Very good, Father, thank you," Rego replied quietly.

He continued to help the other passengers in his section sit down at their tables. He went back over to the wall and stood and waited. Hector made a quick pass in front of Rego and said firmly under his breath, "No conversations, mister!" Rego gave him a sarcastic smirk behind his back.

All of sudden, Lars grabbed Rego's sleeve. "Come on, we have to serve the plates tonight." Hector had made a last-minute decision to serve all the passengers at their tables so they wouldn't have to stumble around the buffet line. So, all the servers immediately lined up in the kitchen to grab large trays of pre-prepared plates to carry out to each table.

Rego watched as each server grabbed a large tray and hoisted it up and quickly carried it out. "This should be interesting," he muttered under his breath.

Erik hoisted a tray above his head, "Let the circus begin," he said striding out.

"Enough chatter," Hector said above the laughs. "Keep it moving. Use caution, everyone!"

Each server carefully walked out to each table. Another server quickly set a tray holder at each table and the server set the large tray down upon it. All around the room, servers danced with their trays on the ever-swaying floors beneath them. It was a carnival of folly to watch them all balance the trays as they made their way between the tables. Despite the swaying ship, not one server dropped their tray and the meal went on without a hitch. Hector was near fainting at the end, but his crew had finished the evening with success.

Rego could hear laughter and music playing down the hallway as he approached the crew room. Inside, all of his co-workers unwound from the hectic night and stood or sat around chatting, eating, and sipping on cold sodas. An old radio on a ledge played some rock and roll. Erik saw Rego walk in the room.

"I've got good news and bad news, buddy," he said taking a long drink from a soda bottle. "The bad news is we're stuck."

"What do you mean?" he asked curiously.

"We're stuck off the coast of one of these islands, the one we were supposed to stop at, Mont something," he said clumsily. "There's some tropical storm in our way and the captain has parked us in a bay to wait it out. They think it is going north of us towards Cuba. We're stuck here until it goes by."

There was a small deck off the crew room, but Rego could not see anything from the small window. It was too dark, and the storm was very rough. "What the hell is the good news?" he asked.

Erik put his hand on his shoulder, "We've got a radio, my friend. And we are in the middle of an island chain. The match starts in ten minutes!"

Rego's eyes widened. "The World Cup? Brazil? We get to listen? You've got to be kidding!"

"Nope, we're already picking up stations with music. One of these islands has got to be carrying the match," Erik said confidently.

"Who did they draw? Do you know?" Rego was very excited.

"The Czechs," Erik answered smartly. "Should be a good one."

The two men and others pulled chairs around the radio while another feverishly turned the dials on the radio, trying to tune in anything. The radio crackled in the storm, but a faint signal started to come through in Spanish. He put his ear closer to the radio. He started waving his hand to the people crowded around the radio.

"Shush, quiet, I can't hear," he said frantically. He listened to the voices on the broadcast: *"The players have taken the field here in Guadalajara and the crowd is on their feet..."*

"I found it!" he said loudly. The whole room cheered and then quieted down and listened to the broadcast intently. He turned the radio as loud as he could. Rego slapped his hands together and leaned forward in his chair to listen to his country take on Czechoslovakia in the World Cup.

As the match played on the radio, other crew members came in and out of the break room. Lindsey walked in with several of the girls to see all the men listening to the game.

She shook her head, "I can't believe it, they're all in here listening to soccer." She shrugged her shoulders and pulled up a chair. "Beats sitting on a rolling bunk." One of the guys started handing them sodas to drink as they all listened to the game.

As the game played on, cheers would ring out after each goal was scored. Brazil scored a goal, but then the Czechs answered with their first goal shortly afterward. The second goal for Brazil was scored by none other than Pelé. Rego stood and danced around the room in celebration. Bottles of soda clinked together, and people even clapped.

At the intermission, people stretched their legs and peered out the windows to see how the storm was coming. The waves lashed the sides of the ship hard as they knew the storm was still nearby. Lindsey watched Rego as he walked around the room excitedly. She wanted to talk to him, but it was difficult with so many people around and her poor command of the Spanish language. She smiled though, when he noticed her and tried to catch his attention. From time to time, her eyes would catch him looking over at her.

The roar of the crowd was heard when a third goal was scored as the radio announcers enthusiastically called the game. The Brazilians scored yet another goal and soon the game was well in hand. Rego smiled triumphantly and was so happy he was able to hear his country's first match. The Brazilians triumphed over the Czechs, four goals to one.

After the match was over, they tuned in some music and couples began to dance to the sounds of island music. Rego sat with a soda in his hand next to Erik and savored the victory while watching the people dance. Erik got up and started to dance with any girl he could find.

Rego began to think about Rosa again. Dancing was something they did quite often at street dances. She was very good at the Samba and Cha-cha and had taught him how to dance them. He knew she was happiest on the Saturday evenings when it was warm, and they would dance for hours out in the streets with music playing and crowds everywhere.

Lindsey came and sat next to Rego. "Hey there, sport, fancy meeting you here." Rego smiled at her. He wished he knew what to say to her. He decided to compliment her and hoped she would understand.

"Esta noche pareces muy hermosa," he said politely to her.

"Muy hermosa, me?" she said blushing. "Oh, thank you." She sat and watched the people dancing. She was dying to get up and dance with them. She finally looked at Rego and motioned to the dance floor. "Do you wanta dance?" Rego pointed to himself and shrugged his shoulders shyly.

"Yes, *you*," she said laughing. He nodded and stood and held his hand out to her. She grabbed his hand and jumped from her chair and they went out to the dance floor.

They started to dance the Cha-cha with everyone else. Rego was impressed with how well she danced. Lindsey was equally impressed that he knew the right steps. Erik and his partner danced by the two of them.

"You, sly *dog*, you," he called out to Rego. Rego shook his head and smiled back at him. He was having fun dancing again with all his new friends.

It was close to midnight and the storm had calmed down outside, but the ship stayed anchored in the bay off the island of Montserrat. The party was winding down, but a few people were still dancing. Rego and Lindsey were slowly dancing the tango, but Rego had a hard time remembering the right steps. Lindsey looked lovingly at him as they danced. Rego tried not to notice, but he could feel her eyes on him as they danced. Her hands were soft in his and her perfume was intoxicating. He could feel her getting closer to him. Just then, Hector walked into the room with his arms crossed. The music stopped abruptly. Rego felt almost relieved to see him. He could tell Lindsey was really warming up to him.

"If any of you people are on breakfast detail, you had better not be in here," Hector said firmly. "Time to wrap it up, people." The crew moaned in displeasure as they started to head back to their cabins.

"Thank you for dancing with me," Lindsey said sweetly to Rego. She was hoping he would walk with her back to her cabin, but his cabin was just down the hallway. Hers was on the deck below. Besides, he felt too nervous and didn't want to do anything more to lead her on. She squeezed his hand and smiled, then walked back to her cabin. Rego took a deep breath and exhaled long and hard after she left. He wiped his tired eyes and picked up a few empty soda bottles to throw away on his way out.

Chapter 13

The next morning, the sun began to rise from behind the clouds, as the *Montenero* sat near Sugar Bay at Plymouth, Montserrat. It was a beautiful sunrise after the storm, and many people were out on the decks watching as it rose over the coastal city. The tall palm trees fluttered in the warm breeze and the peacefulness of the tiny Caribbean island emerged to show itself after the night-long storm.

Many passengers were eager to disembark and explore the tiny island, but they could not. The captain had intended to arrive sooner the day before but was slowed by the storm and decided to wait it out on the west side of the island. An announcement was made, throughout the ship, apologizing to the passengers for not being able to visit Montserrat. It would take too long to board the tenders and go to the island and back again. They had to get back on schedule for the Mediterranean.

Rego finished his morning duties and was walking on the main deck, taking in the view of the small island. He, too, wanted to explore the island and was disappointed when he heard the announcement. The ship soon sounded the horn and slowly started to head south around the tip of the island. He watched as they slowly rounded the coastline. Mountains rose from the middle of the island and cascaded down with dark flowing green, all the way to the sandy seashore. *What a beautiful area this is*, he thought to himself. He dreamed of taking Rosa here one day. *She would just love this.*

The *Montenero* slowly pulled away from the island chain and Montserrat grew smaller and smaller behind them as they journeyed onward. Rego walked along the wooden walkway, taking in the sun, when a group of people passed him coming from the other way. One of them was the priest from the table in his section. The priest smiled as he saw Rego walking towards them.

"Ah, there is our faithful steward," he said warmly. "I am glad you are able to take some time and enjoy this fine sea air."

"Good morning, Father, nice to see you again," Rego said.

"Do you mind if I walk with you?" Fr. John asked.

"Not at all," responded Rego. "My name is Rego," he said extending his hand. "Are you traveling with the Americans?" He was hoping he wasn't prying too much.

"They are old friends of mine from when I studied in America. I am the ship's minister during the summer months. I asked them to join me on this trip," the priest explained. "I'm originally from Barcelona, where the *Montenero* is based. I will go back home with the ship after we leave from Athens."

"Sounds like a great way to live in the summer," Rego said. "I am from Brasilia."

"I see. You are far from home as well then," Fr. John said concerned. "My friends all appreciate how hard you work in the dining area. You are very good at what you do."

"Ah, it's just a job to get from here to there. Thank you, though," he said as they walked along. "I don't think I could do this all the time."

"So, you are just working on the ship, so you can get across to Europe?" Fr. John asked.

"Yes, I thought it would be a great way to see the world, live a little," he said looking at the bright blue sky. "It's very relaxing here. No one chasing you around."

"You have people chasing you?" Fr. John asked with a chuckle.

Rego looked quickly at him, "Oh no, nothing like that. I just mean there are no bosses looking after your every move. It's nice."

"So, do you plan to go back home someday?" he continued asking.

"Oh yes, but not until I am ready. Not until I find what I'm looking for," he said, almost thinking out loud.

Fr. John nodded. "Yes, we are always looking for something or running from something. It's human nature. I remember when I was your age. I wanted to see the world too. That's what brought me to America. I don't even remember what it was that prompted me, I just left one day and searched the world over."

"What did you find?" Rego asked curiously.

"I found that the Good Lord wants us to see new things and experience other ways of life." He paused for a moment. "But I also learned that it is important to not forget who you are and what your duties are. Once your journey through the world is complete, you must accept that the real journey is where you began."

"And where is that?" he asked.

They stopped walking and the priest looked at him and pointed towards his chest. "Right here at home, where your heart is. Have faith in the Good Lord, and He will always lead you back to the journey that matters. The journey of a man." They continued walking for a while longer until Fr. John began to get tired.

"This looks like my stop," he said with a smile. "It was a pleasure finally getting to talk with you, Mr. Rego. I don't want my friends to think I fell overboard." Rego smiled at him.

"Same here, Father, thank you. I enjoyed talking with you too." Rego meant it too.

Fr. John turned to walk away but stopped and turned around. "The chapel is down on D deck if you ever want to drop in. We have services this Sunday. The crew is always welcome to come as well as the passengers." Rego nodded to him. "Don't forget, my son, the door to God's house is always open." With that, he turned and headed downstairs.

Rego watched as he disappeared down the stairs. He thought about what he had said. It did make him feel better. He thought about how he had stopped going to Mass after his grandfather had died. He started to realize that he had neglected a large part of his life. Or perhaps just ignored it. One thing that was for certain, however, was that he knew that an unseen hand was guiding him through his journey and watching over him at every turn. He began to see that the whole journey became less and less about the satchel and more about him finding his way back again. He thought about his uncle whom he hadn't seen in so many years. Perhaps it was his way of helping him come to grips with so much loss.

Rego leaned against the railing and watched the sea flow past. *Sometimes, you need to step back to see the whole picture and see where your place is in the world,* he thought to himself. *And sometimes, you just need a vacation.*

The days passed as the *Montenero* crossed the Atlantic Ocean. The crew grew weary and many of the passengers grew restless. It was the leg of the journey that they all knew would be long and it was compounded by the fact they were not able to disembark at Montserrat.

The crew did its best to keep the passengers entertained as they sailed on. Lindsey held games in the ballroom during the day for the passengers to participate in. They played bingo, trivia games, bridge tournaments, and even talks by individual passengers on topics of interest. The captain would announce news to the ship that he acquired using the ships powerful transmitters. He related important news from around the world, including the latest results from the World Cup. Italy, England, Romania, Peru, West Germany, and Uruguay had all earned triumphant victories in their respective groups. Brazil had even won their second match which was against England, one goal to zero.

Rego stepped out of the bathroom into the hallway. He almost reached the door to the cabin when Bolo came bounding down the hallway, just finishing up his shift at lunch.

"Another lunch forced down their throats," he said sarcastically. "I swear the lunches are becoming shorter and shorter now. These people are never hungry anymore. I don't even know why they show up?" He slapped Rego on the back as he opened the cabin door. "I'm up for some ping-pong, what do you say?"

Rego dove onto his bunk. The long voyage across the sea was starting to wear on him. "I guess so," he said exhaling very tiredly. "I'm not too good at it though."

They walked to the promenade deck and found a ping-pong table tucked away in a corner by a stairwell. They found some old paddles in a box sitting on a nearby bench. The box had two old ping-pong balls in it as well. Bolo bounced over to one side of the table and Rego walked slowly to the other side.

"So, what do you do?" Rego asked showing little interest.

"It's just like tennis," Bolo said stretching his arms and shoulders.

"I don't know tennis either," Rego said staring at his paddle.

"You just hit the ball, man." Bolo held up his paddle and the ball. "You ready? It can only bounce once each time." He served the ball and the ball bounced three quick times and Rego swatted at it and hit nothing.

"This ball is too small, I can't even kick it," Rego complained. He fetched the ball rolling on the floor.

"You serve it to me," Bolo suggested. Rego held up his paddle awkwardly and slapped the ball to the other side and Bolo quickly retuned the serve. The ball went sailing past Rego's paddle again.

"Ah," Rego protested. "This bat is too short too."

"It's a paddle. Try again," Bolo said getting frustrated with him.

Lindsey came walking down the stairwell. "What's going on down here, guys?"

Bolo shook his head. "Well, I wanted to play some ping-pong but instead I am watching Rego pick up the ball every five seconds. What's shakin' Lindsey?" Rego was impressed with Bolo's command of English.

"I just did bingo with a room full of screaming old ladies," she said plopping down on the bench.

"Sorry I missed it," he said laughing.

Determined, Rego served the ball again and Bolo returned it with ease. He finally hit the ball back, but it sailed into the net. He picked it up and served it again. The ball ended up in the net again. Bolo served the ball to Rego and it ended up in the same place again. Lindsey observed the game with a dumbfounded look upon her face.

"This is pathetic," she said with a pained expression. "I can't watch this." She grabbed a paddle from the box and leaped to the end of the table next to Rego. "Let me show you how it's done, soccer man."

Rego stood watching as she and Bolo expertly hit the ball the back and forth with little effort. He shook his head and slowly walked over to the bench and watched them play. He watched as Bolo finally met his match.

"Let's play a game," Lindsey challenged him. "You start."

"You're on," Bolo accepted. He served the ball and the game began with Lindsey beating him easily.

"Damnit!" Bolo shouted as the ball went whizzing by him again.

Rego smiled as his roommate was schooled in ping-pong. "Sitting here and watching is much better," he mused.

"Yeah, yeah," Bolo retorted. "She's just getting lucky."

"Of course," Rego said with a laugh. Lindsey was enjoying herself, watching Bolo run after every winner she hit.

Rego began staring past the ping-pong table, out to sea. He stood up to get a better look, something had caught his attention. He pointed out to sea and said in English, "Look!"

Lindsey and Bolo stopped their game and looked in the direction he pointed. Far in the distance, a group of islands, spaced far apart from one another, could be seen. "Hey, I wonder what those islands are," Lindsey said excitedly.

Bolo nodded, he had seen these islands before. "They are the Canary Islands. They are just off the coast of Morocco." He smiled at Rego. "We are getting closer!"

Rego looked with fascination. "Really, Morocco?" he asked curiously. Lindsey stared at them too. She had never seen them before either. Rego looked over at Bolo who was waiting for Lindsey to come back to the table. "Tell me about Morocco. Have you been there?"

Bolo shook his head. "No, but I hear it is a wonderful place. Lots of history. And excellent craftsmen." He shot a glance at Lindsey, "Can we get back to the game now?"

Lindsey answered with a smile, "You mean me whipping your butt? Of course."

"What kind of craftsmen?" Rego asked.

Bolo and Lindsey started hitting the ball back and forth again. "They are known for their excellent work with leather," Bolo said. "It is sold all over the place. When we stop in Gibraltar, there will be lots of markets. The Moroccan traders come across the straits to sell their leather goods there. It's very interesting to see."

Rego was intrigued. He thought he could take what little pay he had been given and look for a gift for Rosa. He wanted to get something for her from one of these faraway lands. He was certain he would find something nice in the leather markets. "I'd like to see these markets," he said with much interest.

Bolo nodded his head, hitting another ball back to Lindsey. "Well, you'll get your chance then, we should be getting there soon. Probably tomorrow. I'm sure everybody will be getting off the ship when we stop there."

"I love to stroll around the markets. I know I'm going." Lindsey said, smacking another winner past Bolo. "Game over, you lose!" She smiled at Bolo in triumph.

"Beginner's luck," Bolo said embarrassed. "Hey Rego, we're having another party tonight after the dinner shift. A little pre-arrival party. You ought to come. You kids can do some more dancing," he said with a wink.

Lindsey put her paddle in the box sitting next to Rego. "I'll be there," she said smiling at him. She headed back up the stairwell. "Nice game, loser!" she shouted down to Bolo as she disappeared up the stairs. Rego rested his chin on his fist and grinned at Bolo. Bolo smiled back at him very mischievously.

The cleanup of the evening meal was winding down and some of the crew slowly started making their way to the crew area break room. The music was playing and a few of them finally sat down to have a bite to eat. Rego sat on a bench, eating some leftover roast beef on a sandwich. Erik sat next him holding a cold bottle of soda to his forehead.

"Oh man, those rich fogies give me such a headache," Erik said wearily. "And that old lady Mrs. Johnson kept pinching my butt every time I refilled her wine glass. Man, that lady can drink."

Rego smiled as he kind of listened to him. He was in deep thought as the ship neared the Mediterranean. He became more and more anxious as they got closer to the port of Malta. *What will happen when I step off the ship*, he thought to himself. *Will the agents be there? Will I find the Sister of St. Paul? Does such a person even exist or perhaps is it symbolic of something else?* His mind ached with too many questions and no answers at all.

"Speaking of girlfriends," Erik said cleverly. He elbowed Rego who snapped back into reality. Lindsey walked into the break room, carrying a bottle of soda. Rego slumped in his seat and stared at his sandwich. She walked right past them, trying to get Rego's attention, but he never looked at her. Erik looked at him puzzled. "What's with you?" he asked him.

Rego shook his head and picked at his food. "I guess I'm not too hungry right now."

The music continued to play, and some people started to dance. Erik and Rego took their plates to the kitchen and then came back into the break room. They stood and watched as the people danced. One of the girls across the room made eyes at Erik.

"Well, buddy, gotta run. Duty calls," he said winking his eye at him. He strolled across the room and led the young girl to the dance floor.

Rego could see Lindsey talking across the room. He knew he would have to face her sooner or later. He knew she would want to dance, but the whole journey he was on was starting to wear him down. He knew the challenge and purpose of it all still lie ahead of him. It was difficult to muster much enthusiasm for the party.

He took a deep breath and walked through the dancing couples and over to where Lindsey was standing and talking to her friends. He put a smile on his face and snuck up behind her. Lindsey turned around and smiled when she saw him.

"Hey stranger," she said turning away from her conversation. "What brings you over my way?" Rego smiled shyly at her and motioned to the dance floor. He held up his arm to escort her to the dance floor. She curtsied with a playful smile and took his arm and followed him.

They danced to every song, and when they played the slow songs, she wrapped her arms around him and held him close. She wished she could talk to him more, but she decided she was content to just be able to dance and be close to him. She wanted him to kiss her very badly, but as always, he just smiled and held her close as they danced.

They decided to leave the party and go walking for a while on the main deck. The stars were out brightly and blanketed the sky. She looked up at him lovingly as they walked but he just stared out into the night. She knew his mind was elsewhere, and she was frustrated that she couldn't talk to him about it.

"It's so nice out tonight. I can't believe we're getting closer to Greece. I can't wait to get there," she said as they walked. She talked some more as it made her feel more at ease, even though she knew he didn't understand.

"I don't know what I'm going to do when this trip is over," she went on. "Maybe I'll spend more time in Athens, I don't know. I'm not ready to go back home, though. I love seeing the world."

They stopped and leaned against the railing. She was becoming more and more impatient with their language barrier. "I wish I knew what you were thinking. I wish I could get inside that head of yours. Or at least knew some Portuguese," she laughed at herself, as she sweetly brushed her hand through his hair. She pulled herself in closer to him and bit down on her lower lip. "Don't you want to kiss me?" she whispered softly to him. He met her whispers with a soft stare and silence. She looked down at his chest and her heart began to crumble.

He looked away from her feeling like an idiot. He knew what she wanted, he honestly wanted to kiss her too. He cared deeply for her, but the timing was awful. He knew it wouldn't be right to go any further. She couldn't look at him. Her hands clenched in frustration as she lightly slapped her fists against his chest, shaking her head and sniffing her nose.

"I'm such a fool. Can't you see how I feel about you?" she said sobbing softly. He held up his elbow for her to take his arm. She looked down in sadness. She gazed at him and wiped a single tear from her cheek and sniffed again. She sadly took his arm and he continued walking with her down the deck.

He walked with her down the narrow hallway and then stopped in front of her cabin door. She turned and stared at the door knob. She gathered her courage and then finally spoke softly with her back to him. "You have a girlfriend, don't you?" He tried to look over her shoulder as if he didn't hear what she said. Then she tried her best to speak in Spanish. "La novia? En Brasil?" she asked, turning slightly around, still looking down. She finally lifted her head. She had tears running down her face. Rego felt ashamed. He felt terrible seeing her like this. He put his hand to her face and wiped the tears away.

He finally nodded and said softly, "Sí."

She wiped the rest of her tears from her face and straightened up. She gathered all her courage to accept the reality. Then she smiled faintly and nodded. She opened the door to her cabin and started to walk inside but she stopped. "She's a lucky girl," she said, staring at her door. Then she stepped inside and closed the door.

Rego stood in the hallway staring at the door. He hated that the night had ended this way. He felt ashamed that he had led her on, but the communication gap made it difficult. He tried to rationalize it all in his head, but he knew actions spoke louder than words.

He started to turn and walk back down the hallway when suddenly the door opened. Lindsey ran out and threw her arm around his neck and pulled him close and kissed him long and passionately. After a few long moments, she pulled her lips away and quickly slipped back inside and shut the door behind her. He stood dumbfounded in the middle of the hallway for what seemed like hours. He smiled at her courage and decided it was as good a time as any to turn and walk away.

Chapter 14

Early the next morning, the passengers emerged from their cabins to find they were sitting at port in Gibraltar. A small breakfast service was available if they wished, but most of them were eager to disembark and spend the day in the unusual, but scenic port city.

Rego and Erik waited tables patiently, but the dining room was mostly empty, and the ship felt oddly quiet. Both of them were eager to leave the ship and see the city as well. Soon, all the passengers had left the dining room and they quickly cleaned off all the tables and hurried all the dishes and glasses to the cleaning window. They ran back to the cabin and threw on some civilian clothes and made their way down to D deck to the gang plank.

They were all very glad to get off the ship once again. Rego took in the sights of the large coastal city as he walked down the gang plank. In the distance he could see the huge Rock of Gibraltar standing high, as if a guardian over the entire city. The sun was shining brightly over the Mediterranean waters and the breeze was salty and warm. Streams of tourists and crew members walked the streets, looking through small shops and vendors selling their wares on tables and carts on the sidewalks. Bolo, Erik and a small group of crew members decided to go to the Rock of Gibraltar and tour the old fortress. Bolo had seen it before and wanted to show them the Macaque monkeys that lived around the Rock as well.

However, Rego decided to stay behind in the city and walk around the leather markets. He grew more nervous as the day neared for their arrival on Malta. From looking at the map onboard the ship, he estimated they would arrive there in no less than two days. It had to be long enough stay for him to leave the ship amongst all the passengers, as they had been granted in

Gibraltar. He ran over in his mind all the steps that he must take when he gets there. As they got closer to Malta, the harder it was for him to wait and conclude his long arduous journey.

He walked around and noticed how his legs felt wobbly on the solid ground. He had been at sea so long, he had grown used to the rolling and swaying of the ship underneath his feet. He slowed his pace to regain his composure and adjust his legs. He felt nauseous at times with the uneasy feeling.

He strolled by many tables and carts of Moroccan leather goods. Many of the vendors approached him, holding up belts, wallets and other goods made of leather. He thumbed through a table of decorative coin purses and small pouches. One of the coin purses was dark brown leather that snapped together on the front. The small flap was decorated with a nature scene with the sun in the sky, shining over a large expanse, as if you were staring down from the edge of a cliff. He liked the way it looked, and the fresh leather had a new aroma of freshly polished oils. He smiled and thought it would be a nice gift for Rosa.

Then, on another table, he saw exactly what he was looking for. He picked it up and studied every angle of it. The shape and color were exquisite. He looked it over very carefully and then set it back down on the table. The peddler talked to him in his native tongue, trying to convince Rego to buy it. Rego turned to the vendor and pulled out what little money he had. He looked at the man and holding up the piece he answered, "This one is perfect."

It was nearing five in the afternoon, and many of the passengers lined up to go back up the walkway that led to the ship. Many of them carried paper bags filled with souvenirs and larger items that they carried in their arms. They carried postcards, belts, jewelry boxes, leather jackets, bracelets, necklaces, and even small Gibraltar flags.

Rego was amazed at all the things these passengers would spend money on. He noticed a newspaper stand at the entrance to the port and scanned over all the different foreign editions. One of them was actually in Portuguese, so he picked it up and handed the clerk the last couple of coins that he had in his pocket. He saw in the bottom corner of the front page, a picture of Pelé celebrating with a teammate. The caption under the photo read, *"Brazil celebrates third World Cup victory, 3-2 over Romania."* He smiled and nodded very proudly. He carried his gift, wrapped up in an old, worn brown paper bag. He made it onboard and went straight to the cabin to lock it away. He quickly donned his uniform and headed to the dining room.

Down in the dining room, the servers feverishly prepared for the evening meal. They had less time to prepare so they worked quickly to be ready by six. At six o'clock, the doors swung open and the hungry passengers streamed inside and headed for the buffet line. Most of them were famished after the long day of touring and sight-seeing in Gibraltar. Rego's section of tables filled immediately and he was soon refilling water and wine glasses.

He approached the table, with the Americans and Fr. John, holding a pitcher of water. All the Americans shouted in unison, "Rego!" Standing across the room was Hector, rolling his eyes as heard the people having fun with their server.

"How's it going, Rego old boy?" Sammy asked patting him on the back. Rego smiled as he rounded the table, refilling the glasses. He stepped behind Fr. John and picked up his glass to refill it.

Fr. John turned in his chair and said, "I saw you in the leather markets today, very nice, wasn't it?" Rego nodded to him. "A splendid choice you made," he said with a smile.

Rego hadn't noticed him while he was looking around the market earlier. He found it curious that he had noticed what he was buying. "Thank you, Father. Did you enjoy the city?"

147

"Oh yes, very much so, thank you. I always enjoy seeing Gibraltar," he said politely. Rego looked to see Hector frowning at him across the room. He decided to leave the conversation at that.

Back in his cabin, Rego sprawled on his bunk and read the Portuguese newspaper. He read eagerly about the latest victory for Brazil in the World Cup. Pelé had scored the first goal of the match, leading them to a close win over Romania. They had reached the Knockout Stage and would face Peru in the quarter-finals, in just three days time. He thought about young Pelé, the little boy he had met in Lima. He smiled when he remembered how he told his father he wanted the Brazilians to win because his favorite player was Pelé. He laughed at the irony of how his own country was now going to play Peru for a spot in the semi-finals. *The whole continent will be at a fever pitch for that one,* he thought. He hated to be missing out on such a big event.

"You coming down for a bite in the break room?" Erik asked him, combing his hair in the mirror. "We might play some poker later on. Lindsey will probably be looking for you," he said with a wink.

"Nah, I want to catch up on the news here," he said flipping through his paper.

"Ok, buddy, suit yourself," Erik replied and headed out the door.

Rego scratched his head and then looked back at his paper. He thought it would be best if he just stayed in for the night. He didn't feel hungry anyway.

The next morning, Bolo and Rego were up on the main deck, playing shuffleboard. Rego seemed more adept at playing this game rather than ping-pong. The breeze coming over the ship was stifling as the ship sliced through the dark blue waters of the Mediterranean.

"What are your plans once we reach Greece?" Rego asked Bolo, shoving a puck down the floor. The puck settled on the number seven section.

"I don't know," Bolo answered. "I'm in no hurry to get back to Lisbon. My father has been riding my ass about taking a job in his factory. He says I'm wasting my time out here." He sent a puck sailing down the floor and smacked Rego's puck off the number seven. "I don't want to work in that damn factory."

"What do you want to do then?" Rego asked.

"I like it out here," he added. "I love the sea, I love the sea air. I love to be free. I think I could be head steward one of these days. I could go anywhere in the world, see more of it." He frowned as another puck sailed wide. "But my father doesn't see it that way. He says you should work hard and support a family and support your country. I love my country and I love my parents, but I'm just not ready to go back yet."

They walked down to the other end of the shuffleboard and gathered up the pucks and started sending them back down the other way. Rego thought about his parents and wondered what it would have been like to have them alive as he grew up. He wondered if he would have ever gone on this voyage if his parents were still alive today. As usual, he didn't have any answers for his thoughts. All he knew was that he missed his grandmother and he missed Rosa. He longed to be with them, especially when they had to go to Salvador for his uncle's funeral.

"What about you?" Bolo asked him. "What are you going to do? You are a long way from home, buddy."

He had stumped Rego with that question. He really was a long way from Brazil now. Rego shoved a puck down the game board and watched it stop on number ten. He looked over at Bolo, "You know, I haven't thought of what I will do afterward. All I've been thinking about is getting there."

"A man that lives one day at a time, I like that," Bolo said with a grin. "You're gonna be alright, my friend." He sent another puck sailing down the floor and smacked Rego's puck off the number ten and onto the 'ten off' space. "But you're lousy at this game too."

Night came and Rego stood on the main deck, leaning on the railing and staring into the darkness. He could hear the waves crashing by as the ship sailed on through the night. He rubbed his eyes and brushed his hair back over his head. *The time has almost come,* he thought to himself.

Down in the break room, the music played, and the young crew members danced and chatted after the dinner shift had ended. Lindsey sat on a chair in the corner, holding a bottle of soda in her hand. She looked all around the room, but he wasn't anywhere to be seen. She stared at the bottle in her hands with a look of pure sadness.

Chapter 15

The next morning, on a Saturday, the *Montenero* neared the port of Valletta, Malta. The captain announced on the intercom that they would be making port at nine-thirty a.m. but would only be there for three hours. The crew was asked to stay aboard but passengers would be allowed to disembark and tour Valletta if they wished.

When he heard the announcement, Rego began to panic. He knew he had to find a way off the ship. He thought frantically as he did his duties during breakfast. Fr. John noticed he seemed pre-occupied with his thoughts as he rounded their table.

"Are you alright, my son?" Fr. John asked him when he stopped beside him.

Rego snapped out of his trance and looked at the pastor. "Oh yes, Father. I'm quite alright. How are you this morning? Going to see the capital city?"

"Yes, I think I will tour around for a bit, perhaps see the Co-Cathedral of St. John and the Grand Master's palace," he said smiling. "The old knights were called The Order of St. John, you know. I thought I should go see what all the fuss is about."

"Hope you have a good morning, Father," Rego said and quickly walked back to the wall. He looked at the clock on the wall and it read eight-thirty. Several tables had emptied, so he began to clear them off. He wanted to be done as soon as possible, so he could plan his way off the ship. He needed to try and blend in with the passengers that were getting off in Valletta.

The dining room was soon empty, and the servers quickly cleared off each table. Rego dropped the last of his dishes and glasses at the window and made his way for the door.

"Where are you going, mister?" Hector demanded as he stepped between Rego and the door.

"I think I'm going to be sick," he responded quickly and pushed past Hector's shoulder. He put his hand to his mouth as he hurried through the double doors. Hector crossed his arms with the clipboard dangling from his hand and shook his head. Erik looked up from his tables and watched Rego leave in a rush.

Rego went down another hallway to get to his cabin from the other side, to avoid going through the kitchen. He stormed into the room, instantly awaking Bolo from his sleep.

"Oh, what the hell, man?" Bolo asked in annoyance, with his eyes closed.

"Sorry, just getting a few things," Rego said hurriedly. He didn't have much to grab. He threw off his uniform and folded it and placed it on his pillow, then pulled on one of the shirts Erik had given him. He checked his hair in the mirror and combed it over as best as he could with his hand. He stared at himself for a second and decided that he needed something to try and disguise himself.

"Bolo, do you have a cap or something that I can use? I'll pay you for it," Rego asked in desperation.

Bolo sat way up in his bunk. "Why the hell are you rushing around?" he asked rubbing his eyes. Rego looked around the room desperately. "Geez, man. I gotta cap hanging over there on a hook. Take it, it's yours. Just stop jumping around!"

Rego seized the cap and threw it on his head. "Thanks Bolo, you're a real pal." He pulled his jacket from under his bunk and put it on the mattress. Then he knelt by his locker and opened it, leaving the key inside the key hole. He pulled everything out of the locker and rolled up the brown paper bag in his jacket, then threw the satchel over his shoulders across his chest.

"Rego, what are you doing?" Bolo asked, staring at him like a madman. "You ditching us for another cabin, or what? C'mon man, what's going on?"

Rego had packed everything. He looked at Bolo with a look of uncertainty. "It's nothing like that, Bolo." He took a deep breath and exhaled long and hard. "It's time to go."

He stood up with his jacket and satchel and gave a quick, faint smile to Bolo and then walked out. Bolo looked at the door with a crazed and confused expression. He shouted from his bunk, "What do you mean, 'go'? We're not supposed to get off here!"

Rego ran quickly down the stairwell to D deck and slowly stepped outside on the walkway on the starboard side of the ship. Several passengers had gathered to watch the ship pull into harbor, so he tried to blend in as much as he could, wearing the cap low on his head.

In the distance, he could see the island of Malta. The white and beige buildings of the cities could be seen clearly in the early morning sun. The villas and flats stood over the dark blue waters and carved their way up the hillside and then out of view. He followed the coastline with his eyes and then spotted a giant, walled fortress. It looked like an ancient castle, floating on the edge of the water. The wall wound its way around a long and vast peninsula. As the ship approached, he could see tiny windows and lookout holes in the ancient walls of the fort that surrounded the capital city of Valletta. A jetty stuck way out in the harbor on the port side with a small lighthouse at the end. On the right was another small lighthouse, just off the perimeter wall of the fort, several hundred meters from the other lighthouse. The opening to the harbor was wide and dark blue, the waters running still and deep. He watched in silent amazement as the ship slowly entered the doorway to the Grand Harbour. He could see the city walls clearly and up close now. The walled fortress rose above the water over a hundred meters. He was amazed and astounded at what kind of history lay beyond these walls. *An ancient fortress in the middle of the sea!*

Rego was tremendously impressed and fascinated at the same time.

A small boat came pushing into the harbor towards the *Montenero*. It had a sign in English that read *Harbour Pilot*. He saw the boat disappear to the port side of the ship. He remembered his first ticket to the ship in Lima and he chuckled to himself thinking about it.

As they neared the docks, Rego could now see beyond the walls and into the capital city. The streets crisscrossed the narrow peninsula, all of them lined with buildings, churches and small shops. The rooftops were covered with TV antennas, plants, clotheslines and narrow ventilation pipes. The city was old, but it was breathing with life. He could hear the sounds of car horns and slow, old truck engines struggling up the rolling hills, and the common sound of bustling streets. He raised one eyebrow and nodded his head. "Busy place," he said to himself.

The ship came to rest next to a long dock outside of the walls of Valletta. Passengers started to make their way towards the walkway that was being raised to the ship. Rego stood in line with the rest of the tourists, slowly moving towards the exit. Then, Rego noticed ahead, at the top of the walkway, Lindsey, dressed in her uniform, answering questions from passengers about the island and things to see. Rego turned his head away as he got closer to her. She was right at the foot of the walkway.

"Yes ma'am, the cathedrals in Valletta are very beautiful," she said smiling to an older woman and her husband. "Be sure to see the museum and the old town center. I hear they have wonderful open-air markets on Saturday mornings."

All of a sudden, she saw a familiar face draw near the exit. Rego no longer tried to avoid her. He looked straight at her and paused at the top of the walkway. "Rego?" she said with wide eyes. "What are you doing here?"

She looked at him with surprise as he reached out his hand to her. The two tourists behind him stood and looked on curiously

154

and nosily. She grabbed his hand and held it for a brief moment. Then, he smiled at her and said in English, "Goodbye, Lindsey." He kissed the top of her hand and let it go. Lindsey stared at him in disbelief and watched him walk down towards the landing.

He reached the ground and made his way towards the pedestrian gates that exited the port. He looked all around the area for the agents, but they were nowhere to be seen. He stood in a short line to show his papers at the customs desk. He showed them his papers and he walked through the gates and up a long staircase to the street level. He looked everywhere, keeping a sharp eye out. *Where are those bastards?* he thought to himself. He looked back one more time at the *Montenero* and could see Lindsey still watching him as he disappeared into Valletta.

The streets of Valletta were narrow and lined on each side with three to four story buildings. Small shops and stores were on every corner. The streets were old but clean and the whole city seemed to be free of any kind of clutter or debris. It was obvious the Maltese took great care in keeping their cities clean.

He knew he had to make his way to the center of the island, so he followed the streets in the most logical direction. He soon found a wider street that appeared to be in the center of the city. He saw the street sign on the side of the building. It read, 'Republic Street.' He walked south along the busy street, hoping to find a way to Mdina, or at least a reliable person he could ask for directions. Some of the shops sold pastry bread and the smells wafted into the streets. When he passed by, it smelled wonderful to him, but still he looked everywhere trying to see anyone following him.

He came to a busy square with café tables setup in the middle of the square. A few tourists and locals sat at the tables sipping tea and coffee and eating the small pastries sold in the nearby shops. He walked between the tables and chairs to get to the other side. He passed by a man dressed in a fine blue suit coat, sipping a cup of hot tea. Before he could pass him by, the man reached up and grabbed Rego's arm and stopped him.

Rego looked down to see Coutier, dressed very smartly this time without his fedora and overcoat. His hair was combed neatly, and his black eye had faded away. Rego stood speechless and in horror next to him. He looked around feverishly for the other two thugs, but they were nowhere to be seen.

"Why don't you sit down, Rego?" Coutier said in a gentlemen-like tone. "There is no sense in running anymore. Let's just sit down and talk this over, shall we?" Rego shook in fear. His first impulse was to run as fast as he could. "I'm not here to hurt you, Rego. I just want to talk with you. Please, sit down." he said politely again. He released Rego's arm and Rego slowly walked backward to a chair opposite of Coutier. He slowly sat down in the small white chair. He stared at Coutier in disbelief.

"You've come a long way, kid, I applaud your grit and determination," Coutier continued. "But it's time to give this up. What you have there does not belong to you. It belongs to the people of Brazil."

"It belongs to my Uncle Enso," Rego finally said with his voice shaking.

"Enso is *dead*," Coutier answered quickly.

"Yeah, and it was you bastards that probably drove him to his grave, too," Rego replied angrily. "Just like you did to Jacomé! That was *you* who killed that poor man. And for what? This stinking leather case." Rego stood with anger in his eyes, holding the satchel out in front of him. Gomes and LaBonne stepped out from behind the corner of the building behind the table. LaBonne had finally gotten rid of his neck brace. Rego glared at both of them.

"You can't run anymore, Rego. This is an island, there is nowhere else to go," Coutier said still sitting at the table. "You can't have what doesn't belong to you." Gomes and LaBonne slowly inched their way toward Rego.

"What are you going to do, shoot me right here in front of all these people?" Rego asked trembling.

"No, all we want is the case. Now please, just sit back down."

Rego gave a firm look to Gomes and LaBonne, and then back at Coutier. "If you want this case, then you fat bastards are going to have to *catch* me." He flipped a chair towards Gomes and LaBonne and took off running through the maze of tables. Coutier slammed his fist on the table amd Gomes and LaBonne threw the chairs aside and took off after him.

Rego sprinted past the entrance of the St. John Co-Cathedral and down a side street that led to the outskirts of the city. Rego had stored up plenty of energy on the ship and was ready to outrun the agents once and for all. He ran like the wind down the narrow streets and alleyways of Valletta. He turned down every which way he could. He tossed his hat aside as he ran and threw his jacket off too. The men were close behind but Rego ran further and further ahead of them, changing direction anywhere he could. He dashed past people and tourists in the streets and then past a post office and even a police office. He ran as fast as he could. He headed up a small hill towards the harbor side of the city, around a bend, then past another church entrance. As he turned a corner and flew past a large iron gate, he noticed a sign that read 'Upper Barrakka'. He found himself in a large multi-level garden terrace with park benches and tables. The gardens provided a spectacular view of the Grand Harbour in both directions. Rego frantically ran down each level of the gardens, looking for a way out. He ran down to a level that was lined with park benches against a short wall, all of them overlooking the view. Some were occupied by tourists and lovers alike, some were empty.

Coutier, Gomes and LaBonne came running into the gardens, looking everywhere for Rego. All of them were gasping for air. "Go that way," Coutier ordered, coughing a wheezing for air.

Rego ran to the far railing and looked over. All he could see was the water, far below the gardens. He turned quickly and froze in his tracks. Gomes stood right on top of him.

"That's far enough, kid," Gomes said, still gasping for air. "There's no way out of here!" Gomes signaled to the other men. Coutier and LaBonne came up behind him quickly. Rego backed against the railing.

"There's nowhere else to go, Rego," Coutier said. "You've made it this far, but it's time to hand it over. Your grandmother wouldn't want you to keep fighting this."

"You leave my grandmother alone. Leave us all alone!" Rego shouted, his voice cracking. He pulled the strap over his head and held the case in front of him. "Don't come any closer!" Gomes stepped forward. "I *said*, don't come any *closer.*"

"It doesn't belong to you, Rego," Coutier said firmly.

Rego glared at him and snarled back, "It doesn't belong to *you*, either."

"I'm taking that case, kid, and that's that," Gomes said smartly.

"Well then, I hope you can fly," Rego said gritting his teeth, and whirled the case around by the strap. The men backed off as he quickly turned to throw the case over the railing. Just before he released it into the air, the sound the three guns cocked behind him. Rego froze in mid-air, holding the case by the strap from his outstretched arm.

"Don't be a fool, kid. It's over," Coutier said stepping up behind him. He held the gun to Rego's head and slowly took the case from his hands. The three men backed off slowly, still pointing their guns straight at Rego. The onlookers on the park benches were horrified. Coutier motioned to his men, "Let's go."

All of a sudden, several more guns cocked behind the agents from the steps above. "Freeze!" a voice yelled to the three men. Standing above them on the steps were ten Maltese police officers, all pointing guns straight at the Brazilian agents. "Drop those weapons, now!" he shouted again.

"Back off!" Coutier shouted back in English. "This is business of the Brazilian government."

"I don't care if you're the Queen Mother herself," the officer exclaimed. "You men drop those weapons and come with us immediately."

Coutier motioned to his men to do as they were told. They all dropped their weapons and raised their hands. The police quickly took them into custody and gathered the weapons and escorted them away.

Rego, and all the bystanders, looked on in shock as the police took the men away. Rego breathed a heavy sigh of relief. His shoulders slumped as he stared at the pavement. His jaw dropped in realization that the chase was finally over. He leaned on the railing and stared towards the view of the harbor. The onlookers started to disperse and talked amongst themselves about what they had just seen. Rego stumbled across the way towards one of the park benches and collapsed on it. He sat with his head leaning against the wall, exhausted. He just stared at the beautiful harbor.

The police hurried the three agents into a holding cell. Coutier cursed and swore at them in his native language and in English, telling them they were making a big mistake.

"You have no right to keep us here!" Coutier protested. "I demand you release us. We are officers of the Brazilian government. We must report back to our superiors immediately. Do you hear?"

"Shut up," an officer snapped at him. "You're not going anywhere until we hear from your government, so pipe down."

The officers thumbed through the paper documents that they confiscated and even inside the leather satchel. Coutier glared at them through the cell bars as they searched everything. After they were done, the officer walked to the cell and handed them the papers and the satchel. "You can have this back. They're all clean."

Coutier grabbed the leather case and sat down on the bunk inside the cell. He quickly opened the satchel and looked inside. He threw his hand inside and searched it all around and came up with nothing. The entire case was empty. He swore under his breath and examined the case all around the outside. There were no letters or initials on the flap at all. His faced looked incredulous as he turned the satchel over and found wording on the bottom. The lettering read in English, 'Made in Morocco'.

Rego sat with his head resting against the wall. Then, he gathered his strength and sat up on the bench. He took a deep breath, then reached down under the bench behind his feet and pulled out the old, worn leather satchel. He sat the satchel on his lap and stared at it. The flap had the faded initials of his late uncle etched on the flap. Slowly, a thin smile appeared on his face.

He had hidden it away under his shirt the entire time before he got off the ship. The other satchel he carried was identical to the one he had originally. He had found the exact same case on the streets of Gibraltar.

The Maltese officer held the telephone close to his ear, keeping his back turned to the agent's cell, listening intently to the voice on the other end of the line. He examined the three handguns they had confiscated from the agents. He looked at one in particular and nodded as he spoke softly into the telephone, "Yes, we have such a weapon, of that very same description, same caliber." He nodded once again, "Yes, from the agent himself." He peered over his shoulder and glanced at Coutier, scribbling some notes down on a sheet of paper. Coutier glared back at him intently. "Very good, sir. Grazie. Ciao."

The young officer put the telephone down and placed the pistols into an evidence box. He slowly approached the holding cell with a smug look upon his face, clutching his rolled-up notes in his hands. "Well, Captain, it appears you are wanted for questioning by your superiors in Brasilia."

"Concerning what?" Coutier answered coldly and uninterested, staring at the stone floor.

"Concerning the murder of one, Jacomé Pascoal."

Coutier slowly turned his stare upwards at the officer. He knew he was finished.

"So, it appears you will be going home after all," the officer said as he turned away, leaving Coutier with a blank expression.

Chapter 16

Rego walked slowly towards the entrance of the city. The market was bustling with shoppers and locals at the city gates. Outside, he saw a large throng of city buses, all painted dark green with white tops. The buses were old but many in number. The terminal was a round outdoor center of activity.

In the center of the outdoor terminal was a huge water fountain, spraying water high into the air. In the middle of the fountain were three large statues of mermaids. All three of them held a large disc above their heads, and out of the disc was the water fountain, spraying high into the air. Rego looked in awe at the huge fountain.

There were street vendors and buses everywhere. All the buses had numbers in the front window on the driver's side and he noticed that all the steering wheels were on the opposite side. It wasn't long before he realized that they were all moving down the left side of the road as they left the terminus.

He only had a few coins left in his pocket, but first he had to find which bus he should take. He had no idea how far it would be to the city of Mdina. He walked up to a man who he thought was a local. "Mdina?" he asked pointing towards the buses.

"Bus number eighty," he said in English.

Rego shook his head not understanding. "Which bus, Mdina?" he asked again.

The man lowered his eyes at Rego, and said slowly, "Eight-zero."

Rego frowned and then finally said, "Sorry, no English."

The man smiled and nodded. He held up his hand for Rego to wait. He pulled a small pad and pencil from his shirt pocket and wrote the number eighty down in large numbers. He held it up for Rego to see it.

Rego smiled in thanks. "Oh, thank you, thank you," he said in his broken English. The old man nodded and laughed as Rego walked off quickly, looking for the right bus.

He finally found a small, old bus with the number eighty in the window. He climbed aboard and stood in front of the driver. "Mdina?" he asked.

"Yes," the bus driver said. "Seven cents, lira."

Rego pulled the coins out of his pocket and showed them to the bus driver. They were left over from Gibraltar. The bus driver looked at them and shook his head, "Lira only, sorry."

Rego held up his hand as he stepped off the bus. "Uno momento, uno momento, por favor," he said hastily and ran back to the market. The driver put his chin down on his hand and waited. He wasn't going to leave for another ten minutes anyway.

Rego quickly ran around the open-air markets, looking for a way to get the Maltese currency. He looked at the table of goods quickly and then spotted something that looked familiar that he thought was perfect. He picked it up and showed it to the vendor and held out his coins. "Enough?" he asked her.

She took two of the coins and smiled and nodded to him that it was. She gave him a ten-cent piece, in Maltese lira, back in change. "Thank you, thank you," he said smiling graciously.

He ran as fast as he could back to the bus and hopped up the steps, gasping for air. The bus driver looked at him tiredly and held out his hand. Rego produced the ten-cent piece and the driver took it. He peeled off a small white and orange ticket and tore it slightly down the middle, then handed it to him. He also gave him three cents back in change. "Thank you, thank you," Rego said smiling broadly. He walked down the aisle and took a seat by himself in the middle.

Soon, the old bus engine roared to life and the driver put it into gear. The bus slowly pulled away from the fountain and down the streets toward the interior of the island.

Rego sat on the bouncing bus that was now full of passengers, staring out of the window at all the sights. Every street was busy and all of them were lined with buildings and more churches. Even though all the towns ran together, he noticed the town names changed every so often as the bus slowly drove on. Sometimes a passenger would reach up and pull a long cord overhead that ran along each side of the bus. A bell would ring above the drivers head and soon he would pull over at the next bus stop. Several people would get off and several more would get on. The streets winded along the crowded coastline. He could see the brightly colored fishing boats in the small harbors along the way. The boats were painted in bright blues, greens and trimmed with yellow and red and they were everywhere in the small bays and inlets. The bus turned away from the water and headed uphill and into old neighborhoods that had wider streets. Children kicked footballs on the side of the streets and in small empty lots and in many ways, it reminded Rego of home in Brasilia.

The names of the small towns passed by as the bus slowly made its way into the center of the island. He saw names like Floriana, Hamrun, Santa Venera, Balzan, and Attard. The houses and apartment buildings became less and less out in the country, and soon he could see small plots of farmland. The crop lands were separated by small stone walls, only a meter high or less. An old man walked behind a rusty plow, tilling up the soil far from the road. Some farms had small groves of olive trees growing on them and beyond the farmland, Rego's eyes fell upon a massive structure in the distance. In the center of the island was a large stadium and it appeared that a match was going on there. He could see crowds of people on the outside of the stadium, slowly making their way to the entrances. Rego was impressed that football seemed to be a very popular pastime here, just as it was in Brazil.

The bus turned down a narrow road that led right towards the giant stadium. Rego saw the sign as the bus turned, it read 'Ta'Qali Stadium'. The driver turned left on another small road before they reached the stadium. Rego strained to see the stadium from the other side of the bus where he was sitting. He soon gave up and sat back down in his seat.

Then, he saw it. High on a hill on a very narrow road, was a walled city. The walls were light brown and grey and very old. Then his spirits soared when the bus drove past a sign that read 'Mdina' with an arrow pointing ahead. He sat way up in his seat and pressed his hands and face to the window. He stared at the ancient city in awe as the bus slowly crept closer. *I can't believe it*, he thought. *I am really here.*

The bus pulled up to its final drop-off point. Everyone on the bus began to get off the bus. The bus stop was still a way's down the hill, a good quarter of a kilometer from Mdina. He could still see the large stadium off in the distance as he got off the bus and stretched his legs, staring at the walled city. He would have to walk the rest of the way, so he threw the satchel over his shoulder and began walking up the steep hill towards the city. His eyes stayed glued on the entrance with its tall gray stone walls. As he neared the gates, a roar from the stadium could be heard. The crowd cheered at the football game, celebrating an obvious goal for the home club. Rego looked at the stadium and smiled. "I like it here, already."

Rego stood in front of the gates to Mdina and stared at them in awe and wonder. *What will I find inside these walls?* This was the moment he had worked so hard far, the moment he had traveled so far to see. He had finally made it. He stepped inside the walled city to see small crowds of tourists milling around the ancient streets. A few locals were around as well, for some still kept their residences here. A man sold flowers to men to give to their sweethearts. Another sold tea and small pastries. Otherwise, it was very quiet and peaceful inside the city.

Occasionally he would hear the roar of the crowd from the stadium, but it was very muted now inside the city walls.

He continued walking down the narrow main road until he came into a small square. A local was passing by, carrying loaves of bread in a basket. Rego stopped her as she passed by, "Do you know the Sister of St. Paul?" he asked. The woman looked at him puzzled. "Santo Paulo?" he asked again.

Her eyes lit up and turned and pointed behind him to a large cathedral on the other side of the square. Above the large door to the church were the words, 'Cathedral of St. Paul'. Rego thanked the woman and slowly approached the church, staring at it with his eyes agape. He stepped inside the large church and saw it was more beautiful than he could have imagined. The paintings on the walls and chandeliers were ornately decorated. He dipped his hand in the holy water and made the sign of the cross as he walked in. An old man, perhaps a caretaker, was hobbling down the center aisle of the church towards the back.

Rego whispered softly to him, "Pardon me, sir."

The man understood his language and answered him, "Yes, my good man?"

"Could you tell me where I may find the Sister of St. Paul?" Rego asked, expecting to hear the worst.

"Of course," the old man said. He pointed to the side of the church towards a stain glass window. The particular window had a figure of the Virgin Mary on it. Rego felt a little discouraged, thinking the old man did not understand him. The old man smiled and motioned towards the window once more. Rego looked closer at the window. Through the glass, he saw some people working outside. Three women, wearing habits, appeared to be working in a garden. Rego nodded to the old man and slowly started to walk out the main door, still staring towards the stain glass windows curiously.

He stepped outside the church and walked around to the left side and peered down a small walkway that led to a tiny courtyard and garden. The three nuns worked happily and quietly, planting small shrubs and vegetables and a few flowering plants. The garden was covered in shade for most of the day and there was a small gate to walk through to get into the small garden area. Rego's heart pounded as he slowly opened the little gate.

"Hello, Sister?" he said softly in his own language. "I was looking for…"

"Rodrego?" the nun asked, astonished. "Is that you, boy?"

Rego dropped the satchel on the ground and his jaw fell open. "You know who I am?" he said in amazement.

Her eyes flew wide open in surprise. She brushed the dirt off her hands and got to her feet. The other two nuns looked on briefly, then went about their work. She walked over to the gate where Rego stood with an awestruck look on his face. The nun smiled at him and couldn't believe he was there in front of her.

"You really do have your mother's eyes," she said. Rego stood dumbfounded. "You don't remember me, I know. You were such a such a young boy when I came to this monastery."

"*You're* the Sister of St. Paul?" Rego asked, still trying to grasp the shock of the situation.

The nun laughed out loud. "Well, not quite. But, I am one of the caretakers of the church that bears his name, though," she said motioning to the cathedral. "I am a member of the Order of Saints Peter and Paul Monastery here at Mdina. One of our tasks is to help look after this old and wonderful cathedral." She looked at Rego and brushed his long hair away from his eyes. "Rodrego, I am your Aunt Lina Botelha."

Rego finally snapped into reality and recognized the face of his great aunt. He threw his arms around her and hugged her tight. Tears ran down his face. He looked at her with a gleeful smile, saying, "Aunt Lina, I should have known. Grandma had always said you were in the old country."

She nodded, "I was, for many years. Then I came to this country about seven years ago." A look of remorse came over her. "I had longed to go back home to Brasilia and Salvador to visit my sister and brother, but the life of a nun is a lifelong dedication to work and serve the Lord. Plus, I hadn't the money to make such a long journey. Now I'm afraid I am much too old to make it that far." She smiled at him again. "Oh Rego, it is so good to see you. You're a young man now!"

"It's wonderful to see you too, Aunt Lina," he replied. "I had no idea what I would find here." His face turned sad all of a sudden.

"What is it, my child?" she asked concerned.

"I'm afraid I have bad news," he answered sorrowfully. "Uncle Enso, your brother, has passed away. I called home almost two weeks ago when I was in Panama. My friend, who looks after Grandma, told me."

Lina stepped away a few steps. She held her crucifix in her hands that hung from her neck. She nodded and looked back at Rego. "God, give him peace," she said. "I knew he had been ill. I'm so sorry, Enso," she said to herself.

"I think he wanted me to give you something," Rego said, picking up the satchel. Aunt Lina looked over at him curiously. "That's why I'm here. Just before he died, he instructed another man to bring this to me and told me to bring it here."

Suddenly, Lina remembered everything. She knew exactly why Rego had been sent so far and what was inside the satchel. She nodded quietly, staring at the satchel. She bit down on her lip and said, "He knew he didn't have much time."

He handed her the satchel and they walked over to a small bench that sat near the wall in the tiny courtyard. They sat down together on the bench. She opened the satchel and took out an envelope that read 'Lina' on the outside. She opened it and found a letter inside. She read it aloud to Rego:

My dearest sister, Lina. If you are reading this letter, our trusty nephew, Rodrego, has just completed an historic journey. I would have come myself, but my declining health has made it impossible now for me to even walk down the street, much less travel across the world. I have missed both of my sisters immensely over the years, and I feel ashamed now for not making a better effort to visit both of you over these years. My wish was to one day, travel across the ocean and visit you in your wonderful home there on Malta. I have always admired your spirit and dedication to the Lord's work. But as the years passed me by, I knew my wish would never come to pass. I was no longer able to fulfill such dreams. That is why I have asked Rego to come in my place, to come and see his wonderful aunt whom I love and miss very much.

She wiped a tear from her eye as she read the letter. Rego consoled her and told her to continue.

You probably already know the other reason why I have sent Rego on such a long and dangerous task. As the oldest remaining member of our family, you have been entrusted with the possession that I have carried all these years, that were handed down to me by our father. You will know what to do with them now.

Now that you have read this, my only wish is to see your pretty face in the house of the Lord when the time comes. You are my loving sister and I always hold you dearly in my heart. Please forgive me for not being able to say it to you in person. With fondest love and memories of you, Enso

She sniffed and blew her nose into her handkerchief. "Thank you, Rego. Thank you for bringing this letter to me." Rego nodded to her. "Now let's see what else is in here, shall we?" She pulled out another envelope. "This one is addressed to you," she said smiling.

Rego took the envelope and opened it. He pulled the letter out and unfolded it. Still dumbfounded, he read it out loud:

My dear boy, Rego. By now, you should have found your long-lost auntie Lina. First of all, let me say how proud I am of you, Rego. You have journeyed the longest anyone has in our family since your brave aunt Lina did so many years ago now. I apologize for being so secretive about the whole thing, but I knew that I could depend on you and I knew you would keep to your word and not look upon the contents of the case. After all, as your auntie can tell you, I do love a wonderful adventure.

"That he does," quipped Lina.

This is a journey that I had always wanted to make and now you have made it for me. I was with you every step of the way, my boy, and I am immensely proud of you. I also apologize if you had some bad company along the way. I'm afraid, that what you now hold is a very prized possession of our lovely government. Well, if you are reading this, then I know you have beaten them and have preserved our family's heritage once again. I know you must be confused about all this, but your aunt will explain everything to you in detail. Please look after your aunt and grandmother Rego, I know you will. For such a young man, you have had to face many sad things. You have had a tough life, but you have always been in the best of care with my sister, Maria. Remember, my son, family will always be the strongest bond of life, and it can never be broken. You are most worthy of what we give to you now. My only hope is that you live a long life and raise a wonderful family of your own and that most of all, you are happy. Maria has told me many things about Rosa. She is very happy for you and she loves the both of you very much. God bless you, boy. And remember I am always there with you, now, and through all your life's adventures. With love and sincerity, Uncle Enso.

Rego sat with the paper shaking in his hand. He took a deep breath and sighed long and hard.

"This is what he left you, Rego," Lina said, pulling the last of the contents of the satchel out. They were documents written in fancy lettering and an official seal at the bottom of all the pages. "This is the title to a large piece of land, Rego, a piece of land in northern Brazil that has been in the family for several generations. It is said to be where the Botelha family settled when they migrated from the old country centuries ago." She handed the documents over to Rego. He stared at them in disbelief. "It is a land that has been unspoiled for hundreds of years, just south of the Amazon region. It is open, vast and beautiful."

"How much land is it, Aunt Lina?" he asked dumbfounded. He had never heard this story ever in his life.

"It's possibly over four hundred acres of unspoiled territory. Some say it is the lost legend of Salamanca," she said with a laugh.

"Ah, everybody knows that is a myth, Aunt Lina. Every kid in Brazil knows that that cave is empty," he said shaking his head.

"Yes, the cave is empty, but the land is not," she added. "For you see, this land is known to be sitting on top of some of the richest oil reserves in all of Brazil!"

Rego's jaw dropped once again. "*It is?*" he asked in shock. She nodded yes to him with a broad smile on her face.

"That is why the government has hounded us for years for this land. But it is not theirs. And the Botelha family has held onto it for generations in spite of them. I've never always agreed with it, but that is the way it has been ever since I can remember. It has been secretly passed down in the family ever since."

Rego couldn't believe his ears. All this time his uncle had been sitting on a virtual gold mine.

"You have to be responsible though, Rego," his aunt warned. "You must make the right decisions now when it comes to this land. But as the rightful owner, the government can never take it away from you." Rego took in every word she said. "And now that my brother has passed on, God rest his soul, I am now the executor of his possessions. That is why he has sent you here. At the end of these documents is the paper I must sign to hand the property over to you. Do you understand all of this?"

"I do, Aunt Lina," Rego answered. He paused for a moment. "But, people have died, Aunt Lina. They killed a man named Jacomé that was delivering this to me. They wanted to kill me too."

Lina shook her head and made the sign of the cross. "The poor man. This is why I have never agreed fully with this. It is true, there are some ruthless people, but they are not all like this, Rego. Those were just greedy men using the face of the government as a mask. You must learn to trust with your instincts. And pray, Rego. The Good Lord will never lead you astray."

She pulled a pen out from inside her habit. "I might be a nun, but I am a prepared one," she said smartly. She signed the last sheet of the documents and placed them inside the satchel and handed it back to him. "I'm so proud of you, and happy for you as well, Rego. You have traveled a great distance and succeeded very well. I know you can handle this next adventure," she said with a smile. He reached over and hugged her.

They stood up and walked out of the garden together. She put her arm around his shoulder. "So, tell me, my young nephew, who is this Rosa I hear about?" she asked with an inquisitive smile.

Rego stood on the walls of Mdina in triumph, looking at a panoramic view of the island of Malta. He tried to take in all the wonders of the tiny country and thought about his entire journey to get there. An overwhelming feeling of pride and humility of his accomplishment washed over him. The view was incredibly inspiring. In the distance, he saw the stadium and beyond that, he saw the small villages lining the landscape. A large domed church rose from one small village, far down the hill from Mdina. Rego shook his head in amazement. "Thank you, Uncle Enso," he said to himself. "It has been the adventure of a lifetime."

Chapter 17

The next morning, Rego attended Mass for the first time in a couple of years. He sat next to his Aunt Lina in the large Cathedral of St. Paul. He stared at the baroque ceiling and the beautiful altar at the head of the church. From then on, he vowed to renew his faith and attend Mass regularly again.

Sister Lina gave him another surprise that same afternoon. The pastor of the town's church was a devoted fan of football and had arranged to have a small television set up at the monastery to watch the quarter-final match of the World Cup between Brazil and Peru. Rego enjoyed the match immensely, laughing and talking with his aunt and the pastor and the other sisters of the monastery. They all enjoyed their time off from their daily chores, and all of them loved to be around Rego's youthful energy and excitement. Brazil triumphed over Peru with a convincing victory, four goals to two. His favorite player, Pelé, did not score a goal, but he made many assists and spectacular plays on the ball that Rego enjoyed just as much. He thanked the pastor for the opportunity to watch the game and to spend time with them.

The following morning, Rego sat in the kitchen of the monastery eating a small breakfast. His Aunt Lina walked in to join him.

"Aunt Lina, what do you call these little pastries? They are delicious!" he asked with a mouthful.

She smiled at him. "They are a favorite dish among the Maltese called pastizzi. As you can see, I love to eat them as well," she said with a laugh.

Rego continued devouring the small pastries. "Oh, I love pastizzi."

Sister Lina sat next to him and put a piece of pastizzi on her plate. She looked at her nephew as he ate, saying, "I have some good news for you, Rego." He stopped eating and looked at her. "The pastor allowed me to phone my sister this morning very early."

Rego put down his breakfast. "You talked to Grandma? How is she?" he asked very concerned.

"She is well. It was so good to hear her voice," she said. "I wanted to let her know that you were here and that you were alright. She was upset with Enso for putting you through such an ordeal, but I assured her that you made it here with flying colors." Rego smiled bashfully. "She misses you though, Rego. And a certain someone else misses you too." His face turned even redder.

"What else did she say?" Rego asked impatiently.

"I've been praying for her and for Enso. She told me that Rosa brought her to Salvador for the funeral and everything was nice," she said with a tear appearing in her eye, thinking about her brother. "He would be so proud of you, Rego." She sobbed a little in her seat. She wiped her tears away and sat up straight. "The good news is that Enso left your grandmother and me what he had left in his savings, God rest him. And we have decided to use most of it to send you back home to Brasilia."

Rego almost felt like he wanted to cry now. He looked at her with his eyes red. "I don't know what to say."

"We'll put you on a nice airplane this time," she said with a wink. "We girls know how to travel." She wanted to see a smile on his face and tried to make him laugh. It worked well. He gave her another huge hug. "You'll be home in no time."

Sister Lina stood by the gate at the small Malta airport. Rego was at a loss for words as he didn't know if he would ever see his great aunt again, so he tried to push those thoughts out of his mind.

"God will always be with you, Rego," she said to him, smiling at him proudly. "Always remember that. And I will always be with you as well." She hugged him one last time. "Thank you for bringing the letter to me. I will always cherish it. Nothing like hand-delivered mail," she said putting another smile on his face.

"Goodbye, Aunt Lina," Rego said smiling. "Thank you for everything. I will never forget you." He started to walk away, but then he gathered up his newfound courage and decided to let his feelings be known. He hugged her quickly again and said, "I love you, Aunt Lina. May God be with you also." She held him tight and then let him go and watched as he walked to the plane. He turned and smiled as he disappeared around the corner.

She stayed at the gate and watched as the plane rolled down the runway and take off into the sky.

Rego landed at the Brasilia airport, the same day Brazil was playing for a spot in the finals of the World Cup. They were facing Uruguay in the semi-finals in what would be another classic match between two South American countries.

He stepped through the gate to see a very familiar face. Rosa smiled broadly when she saw him walk through the door. He walked up to her and put down his things. They just stood and stared at one another. He couldn't believe she was standing in front of him. After all he had been through and the great distances he had traveled, he was finally home. His ordeal was finished. To Rego, seeing Rosa was the greatest moment of all.

"Hey there, pretty eyes," he said smiling broadly. "You're just as beautiful as the day I met you."

"Oh, be quiet," she said with tears running down her face and threw her arms around him. She was overjoyed to see him again. They hugged each other for what seemed like an eternity.

"I have something for you," he said reaching into the satchel.

"After all this time, you better have something for me," she said smiling at him.

He pulled a small object out of his satchel that was wrapped in brown paper and handed it to her. She unwrapped it slowly and pulled it out of the paper. It was the leather coin purse he had seen in Gibraltar with the sun shining over the land. He had bought the satchel instead and left the coin purse behind in Gibraltar, but he made up for it in the nick of time. He had found the same leather purse in Malta before he had boarded the bus for Mdina.

"It's beautiful," she said looking at it. "It looks like something I've seen before."

"Really, where?" he asked curiously. She smiled at him with a clever look on her face.

"You're not going to believe this," she said as they walked out of the airport.

"Believe what?" he asked impatiently. She kept smiling at him as if she had a secret. "What, tell me!" She began to laugh heartily as they boarded a bus back home.

Chapter 18

Rego, Rosa, and his grandmother Maria, stood in the cemetery in Salvador, looking at a headstone. Rego read the name and stared at it with sadness in his heart. It read, *ENSO SANCHES BOTELHA*. A few feet from the Botelha plot was another headstone for Enso's friend, Jacomé Pascoal.

He reached into his pocket and pulled out an old cloth pouch. He opened it and inside was a handful of old coins. They were the coins he had been given by Enso all those years ago when he was a child. He looked at them briefly then dumped them back into the old pouch. He placed the pouch on the headstone.

"Thank you, Uncle Enso," he said looking at the headstone. "You always knew how to make me smile." He knelt beside the stone and put his hand on it. "It was a wonderful journey," he said with a whisper. "Thank you. And thanks to you Mr. Pascoal for helping me. I'm so sorry for what those men did to you."

He stood and put his arm around his grandmother. Maria looked at him and said softly, "Rosa and I have something to show you."

High upon a cliff, they stood staring at a vast panoramic view of beautiful open country. The sun shined brightly on them and the enormous green hills and fields below. The land stretched as far as they could see up against the sky-blue backdrop. It was the land that belonged to the Botelha family and Rego stood and looked at it with awe.

Rosa reached into her pocket and pulled out her new coin purse and showed it to Rego. The picture on the purse was almost the same as the view from the cliff side. She smiled at him as he looked at it with surprise.

"Amazing, simply amazing," he said looking with them at the incredible view.

"So are you, my love," Rosa said and kissed him on the cheek.

They stood and took in the beauty of the vast expanse before them. With satisfied smiles on their faces and a sense of renewal, they took one last look and then headed back home to start the new day.

About the Author

Keith R. Rees has been writing for over a decade now. He has written poetry, novellas, and a few short stories. *The Brazilian* is his first full length novel.

Keith loves the outdoors, golfing, and traveling with his daughter, Isabella. He has traveled at home and abroad. One of Keith's favorite destinations is the islands of Hawaii and Eastern Caribbean.

Keith has never traveled to Brazil but has always been interested in the many cultures of South America. His experiences in college with his brother John, as an exchange student on the island country of Malta, were a great inspiration for the story of *The Brazilian*. Keith and John were students at the University of Malta in the spring of 1988. They returned to Malta once again to visit friends in 2000. He hopes that one day he can show his daughter this wonderful island country.

Keith and resides in Cedar Park, a growing suburb of Austin, Texas.

www.ingramcontent.com/pod-product-compliance
Lightning Source LLC
Chambersburg PA
CBHW051820170626
46807CB00003B/950